'I asked you a question, *señorita!*'

'Oh, all right!' Shelley was bad-tempered now, because he had started it, and it showed. 'I think you'll find that I finish what I start. I've signed this contract, I like this place, and I'll be happy to look after both surgeries as and when you wish me to.'

She stopped, a little breathless at her own cheek. Miguel's voice was suddenly quiet, and his look interested. 'Are the Camerons well known for being plain-spoken, *señorita*, or are you the only one?'

'You must take me as you find me, I'm afraid.'

Dear Reader

We travel again this month, to Spain and Australia in SWEET DECEIVER by Jenny Ashe, and OUTBACK DOCTOR by Elisabeth Scott. We also welcome back Elizabeth Fulton with CROSSMATCHED where American new broom Matt Dunnegan shakes up renal nurse Catherine, and Mary Bowring, who returns with more of her lovely vet stories in VETS IN OPPOSITION. Just the thing to curl up with by the fire as winter nights draw in! Enjoy.

The Editor

Lancashire-born, **Jenny Ashe** read English at Birmingham, returning home with a BA and rheumatoid arthritis. Married in Scotland to a Malaysian-born junior surgeon, she returned to Liverpool with three Scottish children when her husband became a GP in 1966. She has written non-stop since then—articles, short stories, radio talks, and novels. She considers the medical environment compassionate, fascinating and completely rewarding.

Recent titles by the same author:

THE STORM AND THE PASSION
THE CALL OF LOVE

SWEET DECEIVER

BY
JENNY ASHE

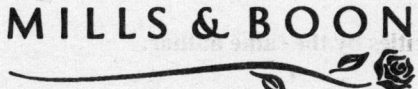

MILLS & BOON LIMITED
ETON HOUSE, 18–24 PARADISE ROAD
RICHMOND, SURREY, TW9 1SR

All the characters in this book have no existence outside the imagination of the Author, and have no relation whatsoever to anyone bearing the same name or names. They are not even distantly inspired by any individual known or unknown to the Author, and all the incidents are pure invention.

All Rights Reserved. The text of this publication or any part thereof may not be reproduced or transmitted in any form or by any means, electronic or mechanical, including photocopying, recording, storage in an information retrieval system, or otherwise, without the written permission of the publisher.

This book is sold subject to the condition that it shall not, by way of trade or otherwise, be lent, resold, hired out or otherwise circulated without the prior consent of the publisher in any form of binding or cover other than that in which it is published and without a similar condition including this condition being imposed on the subsequent purchaser.

*First published in Great Britain 1993
by Mills & Boon Limited*

© Jenny Ashe 1993

*Australian copyright 1993
Philippine copyright 1993
This edition 1993*

ISBN 0 263 78374 X

*Set in 10 on 10½ pt Linotron Times
03-9311-59871*

*Typeset in Great Britain by Centracet, Cambridge
Made and printed in Great Britain*

CHAPTER ONE

PEPE'S Beach Bar was crowded as usual, and the disco music had attracted young people from the holiday village in Santa Barbara del Samana, as well as many locals. It was approaching midnight in the little southern Spanish town, and it was Saturday night on the moonlit Mediterranean. Nobody was even thinking about going home.

Shelley Cameron could never be called strait-laced, but she was finding the atmosphere rather more lively than she was used to back in her little cottage on the sleepy borders between England and Scotland. 'Rosie, don't you think we should go somewhere quieter?' She had to shout to be heard.

Her friend shook her curly blonde head vigorously. 'No way! Just wait till the clock strikes.'

'Why, what happens?'

Just then the clock on the little whitewashed church in the town square began to strike. As soon as the echo of the first chime began to be heard above the laughter, the disco music was toned down, and the dancers on the crowded floor began to move back, leaving a clear space. There was a hushed atmosphere of expectancy. A stool was brought out, and as the last echoes of twelve faded in the warm night air a dark-haired young man with flashing black eyes came and stood alone in the dim light. He was wearing close-fitting jeans, and a loose crimson silk shirt, open at the neck, and he carried a guitar. There were some cheers, shouts of '*Olé!*' and then a chant began — 'Mi-guel-ito, Mi-guel-ito, Mi-guel-ito.'

His smile was white and captivating, and he looked all around, acknowledging the greeting, before putting one booted foot on the stool and slinging the strap of the guitar round his neck. Silence fell. Miguelito strummed a few delicate chords, and began to sing a traditional Spanish folk song in a thrilling deep voice.

Shelley gazed, totally enthralled by his appearance, and by the beauty of his singing. His shadowed eyes roved around, as though he were personally serenading each woman in the room, and Shelley felt a shiver when his glance rested on her neat fair head and blue eyes. She wondered if he really did notice her total absorption with his music and appreciation of his dashing good looks. At the end she took a deep breath, before joining in the rapturous applause, wishing the lights could be turned up. She was sure he was the handsomest man she had ever seen, but it was hard to tell in the shadows.

The next song was a lively one, and very soon some of the local girls, who were dressed in traditional flounced skirts, began to dance, clicking their fingers and tapping their heels, gyrating around Miguelito, smiling at him and swaying their hips with a natural and easy sexuality. By now the atmosphere was electric, as Miguelito went straight into a full-blown flamenco, to cheers and whistles and the clatter of castanets. Bewitched and captivated, Shelley Cameron never wanted to go home. She wanted tonight to go on forever.

'Why did he disappear right in the middle of the fun?' Shelley was disappointed not to have seen Miguelito at close quarters. The girls were walking back under a glorious moon to the holiday complex of Monte Samana, where they were sharing Rosie's parents' villa.

Rosie said, 'That's part of his style. Mystery Miguel, they call him, and he never does more than a couple of songs. Some people say he's a famous opera singer who likes to come incognito back to his roots. I don't know the truth, but does it matter? He's such good fun, and I knew you'd like him.'

'So that's why they didn't put the lights up,' Shelley mused. 'Incognito, eh? How exciting. Well, I hope he comes again next week. I won't be missing it, that's for sure. Am I glad we came out to work for the entire season, Rosie! I think I'll devote my spare time to some sleuthing, to find out where the handsome Miguel really comes from.'

'You won't be the first, I assure you. But try and find out if you want to — you have more spare time off than I do. Your medical centre is only open in the mornings, isn't it?'

'That's what the agent told me when I was recruited. I meet my big chief on Monday morning to find out the details.'

'Lucky thing. I've got to keep the shop open till six at night.'

'Well, the guests always need chemist's things and toiletries, so you should do well financially. Anyway, you get the afternoons off for a siesta.'

Rosie laughed. 'There'd be no use opening. Nobody would come — they'll all be sleeping. I think it's a very civilised Spanish custom.'

'I'll let you know when I've got used to it.' Shelley opened the door of the white-painted villa, and paused to look back across the vista of other villas and apartments, arranged like a real village around little shops, cafés and swimming-pools. 'I'm glad I came, Rosie. And I'm glad I've met Miguel. Somehow I know I'm going to get to know him better.'

'I wouldn't count on it, Shelley. Other girls have had the same idea, but so far he's still Mystery Miguel.'

Shelley didn't argue. But she smiled to herself, as she thought again of the handsome Spaniard with those black eyes full of a sense of fun and adventure, that mane of glossy hair falling over one eye — and his dark brown velvet voice, which had melted her heart a lot more than she admitted to Rosie.

On Monday morning Shelley came down to earth with a bang. The day started well enough—clear blue sky, breakfast on the balcony with Rosie, and that wonderful view across the valley of little houses and shops, up to the gently rolling hills of southern Spain. Today was the start of her contract, which she had signed back home with the agent of the Monte Samana Company who owned this entire complex. She walked cheerfully along the flower-lined pathways to the medical centre, dressed in her working sister's uniform of dark blue dress, neat white shoes and silver-buckled belt. Her long fair hair was coiled demurely at the nape of her neck, and her nails were carefully cleansed of the scarlet polish she had worn on Saturday night. She intended to make a good first impression.

The little clinic was spotless, painted white, with sparkling chrome fittings, stainless steel instruments and pure white fluffy towels. Behind the large mahogany desk sat a tall youngish man with black hair smoothed severely back above regular features, horn-rimmed glasses hiding dark eyes and heavy brows, and an unsmiling face. Slightly put off by his failure to take any notice of her as she entered, her voice was hesitant as she greeted him in her best Spanish. '*Buenos días, señor. Estoy buscando el Médico Rafaelo.*'

'You've found him.' The man finished his notes and looked up. 'I am Dr Rafaelo. You are Sister Cameron, I take it. Welcome to Monte Samana.'

'Thank you.' He didn't sound very welcoming. She tried to be polite. 'It's a lovely place. I'm looking forward to working here.'

He put down his gold pen and looked at her carefully. His eyes were very dark behind the glasses, and his gaze was long and thorough. 'You have very good references, Señorita Cameron. Why did you leave such a good hospital to come and do a holiday job?'

She wasn't expecting the question. It was a personal matter, and she had no intention of telling a snooty foreign doctor about the troubles she had been through with Ken Noakes from Audiology. She didn't want to sound rude, so she smiled her sweetest smile and said, 'I thought I'd already got the job, Doctor. Do I need another interview?'

Was she mistaken, or did the corner of his mouth twitch in a sudden impulse to laugh? No—his voice was grave and deep, with no hint of amusement, as he replied, 'You have the job, yes, but I'm not sure if you realise how much work is involved.'

With her usual brisk matter-of-fact smile, she said, 'That's what I'm here for, Doctor. I'm sure you're going to tell me.'

'Show you, you mean. Come with me, please.' He stood up, revealing a surprisingly young body dressed in dark trousers and a fitted striped shirt with short sleeves. Somehow that lithe, muscular figure reminded her of somebody. . . He wore no tie, but the effect of his neat sleeked-back hair and thick-framed spectacles gave him the look of a rather stern and learned professor. He led the way to the outer office, which had been empty when Shelley arrived, but where now sat a sylph-like creature with a cloud of dark brown curls, and very heavily made-up eyes. Dr Rafaelo paused and said to Shelley, 'This is Victoria, my receptionist.'

The two girls greeted each other, but Dr Rafaelo allowed no further chat. 'Come along, *señorita*. Victoria, we are going to the village clinic. If anyone needs Sister Cameron, please telephone, and I'll run her back.'

He gestured towards a rather battered little jeep parked by a hibiscus hedge at the roadside. 'Get in. It isn't far.'

'Village clinic?' queried Shelley.

'Santa Barbara village. Part of your duties, Sister Cameron.'

Shelley didn't mind, but it would have been polite to let her know beforehand that she had to run two clinics instead of one. 'No problem, but if you want me in the village don't you think I'd better get some transport of my own? A bike or something?'

'It won't be necessary. I will be in the village on most days. It is only when I am on leave that you do both, and you can use the jeep then.'

'Oh.' He was very unbending, this young boss of hers — not even a smile, and his speech was more like that of a headmaster than a colleague. Yes, he reminded her of a stuffy headmaster she had once had, someone who found fault with everyone, however much they tried. Dr Rafaelo so far was proving a bit of a flop. But these were early days, and Shelley wasn't a quitter.

There were no pavements in the little village of Samana, four or five miles from the complex, and chickens and goats wandered idly along the dirt roads, scavenging for scraps. The little houses were small single-storey buildings, with painted shutters closed against the heat of the morning sun. Old men and women sat in the shade of the doorways, chatting and drinking black coffee. Some women did embroidery, while ragged children played noisily around the skirts of easygoing mothers and grandmothers.

Shelley said thoughtfully, 'This is the way real people live. Those guests up in the holiday village are nothing like these people, Doctor. Why are you in charge of clinics in both places?'

'It's my choice, Sister Cameron. Come, let me show you the surgery. After we've seen the patients, I'll tell you more about them over a drink.'

His surgery was simply one of the little stone cottages. Inside were a couple of benches, and several villagers were sitting patiently waiting for him, while an old man sat at the door smoking a smelly little pipe. Briskly, in his headmaster voice, Dr Rafaelo introduced Shelley. She spoke Spanish a little, enough to understand what was going on, although at her interview she had been told that all her patients would be British.

The ailments were minor—a toothache, a jellyfish sting, a child with stomach-ache, and a youth whose broken arm was ready to have its plaster removed. But Shelley was fascinated by the lives that lay behind the complaints. The man with the sting made his living trawling for prawns, and fishing for *mero*, which he sold to the holiday village cafés, for a better price than he got from the locals. It was lucky that there was a large fish market nearby, where the ordinary people could buy cheaper fish. The man offered to take her out in his boat one day, to show her how to catch *mero*. Dr Rafaelo merely said, 'Sister Cameron will have no time for fishing, Pablo. Anyway, when are you going to tell Abuelo Freitas to stop smoking that terrible pipe? I'm sure the smell would put Lina off.'

When they had all been seen to, and no call had come from the complex, Dr Rafaelo summoned Shelley to follow him. He didn't lock the little surgery. She followed him out, turning to see if the door had a number. It didn't, but its flaking paint bore a hand-scrawled name—'Miguel Rafaelo'. He strode along the centre of the main street, and Shelley, with her shorter legs, had to run to keep up with him. He led her to a shady café, where small tables were set out in the shadow of some tall plane trees, whose leafy patterns fell over the white tables. '*Cerveza, María.*' He turned to Shelley. 'Beer? Or lemonade?' It was almost the first time he had sounded civil. It was ironic that her fussy and dictatorial chief had the same Christian name as the exciting young singer who had so caught her imagination last Saturday. It was probably a common name here.

She waited to see if he would explain anything about himself, but he simply sipped his cold beer in silence, idly watching a group of children playing see-saw with a plank of wood over a tree stump. She said quietly, 'Do you come from Samana?'

Miguel Rafaelo didn't turn to look at her, and she continued to study his rather elegant profile while he talked. 'My grandmother does. I was born in Madrid — that's where I studied my medicine. I spent two years in Washington trying to be a surgeon, but I couldn't settle in the States.'

'So you came back to work here? What made you choose to work for the holiday complex? From what I see, you're happier with the local people than with the staff and guests back there.'

He gave her a flicker of a glance. 'You're perceptive, *señorita*. I didn't choose to work at the complex. I own it.'

'What?'

For a moment Shelley thought there was another gleam of amusement behind those glasses at the shrill tone of her exclamation. He repeated the words. 'Monte Samana belongs to me. It was my brainchild. After I came back from America, I decided to go into business, you see, and naturally tourism is the one business that won't fail — not with our climate, and with the lovely beaches around Samana.'

'Then why —— ?'

'Why work as a doctor as well? Because I would be very bored if all I did was administration. Incidentally,' he leaned forward, and she noticed that his face was smooth and tanned, and rather handsome behind those glasses, 'incidentally, I don't go round telling everyone that I'm the managing director. You'll keep it to yourself, Sister Cameron?'

'Oh, yes.'

'I hope so. Now, do you think you can help me to look after both surgeries? You are free to say no. I do find that most people who come out here on short contracts are only looking for a paid holiday. If that's the way you think, then I'd rather know now than later.'

She sat back, and looked at him directly. 'You're very cynical, you know, Dr Rafaelo. I get the impression that you don't trust many people. In my experience, I find that you get what you expect in life, and if you trusted people more, you would probably get more trustworthy staff.'

'Your experience? You are five years younger than I, *señorita*, and you have spent all your life in one place. How can you even mention experience to someone like me? Anyway, I didn't ask you for a lecture! I asked you a question, *señorita*, and I'd like a straight answer.'

'Oh, all right!' Shelley was bad-tempered now, because he had started it, and it showed. 'I think you'll find that I finish what I start. I've signed this contract, I like this place, and I'll be happy to look after both surgeries as and when you wish me to.'

She realised she must be flushed after that, and she stopped, a little breathless at her own cheek. After all, this man was a tycoon as well as a doctor; he must be rolling in money. Perhaps she ought not to have spoken so bluntly, even though he was asking for it.

His voice was suddenly quiet, and his look interested. 'Are the Camerons well known for being plain-spoken, *señorita*, or are you the only one?'

'I can't speak for others, Doctor, and you must take me as you find me, I'm afraid.'

He did smile then, and suddenly she realised that he was capable of charm. What a difference it made to his whole face. He said, 'I didn't shake you by the hand when I met you. I'd like to now. Can we shake on our agreement?'

She held out her hand, and as he took it, he took off his glasses, so that she looked directly into his dark eyes, realising with a start that they were very beautiful and rather disconcerting. 'How do you do?' she said formally.

'I am very well, Sister Cameron, and I thank you for accepting my terms.'

'You haven't said much about terms so far. . .'

'Basically they are simple — you obey my wishes and prevent me being too overworked —'

'I hope your wishes —'

'I hadn't finished.' A look of reproof at her interruption cancelled the warmth of the beautiful eyes. 'My agent told you about the remuneration?'

'Yes.' She looked back with courage, and said boldly, 'It isn't much, but, as you say, we do get a holiday in the sun at the same time.'

'So it is satisfactory?'

'Quite satisfactory, yes.'

'So, Rosie, like a fool I let him manipulate me into working twice as hard as I imagined I would. Monte Samana in the mornings, and Santa Barbara del Samana — the little village — in the evenings.'

Rosie said, 'I suppose you could have refused.'

'Ah, but I like it here. Don't forget I've planned a little job to do outside working hours.'

'Another job?'

Shelley laughed at Rosie's expression. 'My detective work. Mystery Miguel, remember? I'm going to track him down if it's the last thing I do.'

'You won't succeed.'

'I'm a Cameron, Rosie. The more you tell me I won't succeed, the more I'm determined to prove you wrong.' Shelley stretched out luxuriously on the sun-lounger, as the two girls caught the last of the sun beside the pool. Shelley looked up into the dark green fronded fingers of a palm tree, and went on, 'Oh,

Rosie, Rosie, if only my bossy old crab Miguel were as dishy as that lovely singer. Imagine having Mystery Miguel for a boss! What utter and complete bliss.'

'You're getting an obsession with Miguelito, Shelley.'

'And why not? Doesn't it make life interesting? What are we going to wear next Saturday, Rosie? What do you think would make him notice us?'

'Nothing you wear will make a difference, believe me. He's immune to feminine charms. I've seen him before, you see. He's been singing and playing at Pepe's for the last two years, and lots of girls have tried to corner him. He's like the Scarlet Pimpernel— totally elusive.'

'Nobody can be elusive forever.' Shelley was murmuring, as she felt the caressing warmth of the sun turning her pale skin to gold, and allowed a mental picture of Mystery Miguel to linger in her mind.

'Maybe—but longer than your contract, I'll bet. When you're back in your wee stone cottage working for your Dr Ken from Audiology, Miguel will still be here charming the socks off the tourists, you'll see. Anyway, I think he's got a girl—a wife, even. Otherwise he would show more interest—— Oh, God! What's that noise, Shelley?' There was a loud frightening scream from the direction of the children's pool, and Shelley was on her feet and making for the source of the scream before Rosie had finished speaking.

A man lay on the grass, his eyes closed. He was sunburnt, dressed in swimming-trunks. The lifeguard and a distraught woman bent over him, while her toddler stood forlorn and frightened, weeping loudly without understanding what all the fuss was about. Shelley asked quickly, 'What happened?'

'He just collapsed.'

'I'm the nurse. Let me see him.' His pulse seemed normal. She said, 'He's very pink. Have you spent too much time in the sun today?'

The woman looked shamefaced. 'All day.'

'And it's your first day?'

'Yes.'

The lifeguard, Carlos, met Shelley's look, and said, 'Yes, sunstroke, or else heat exhaustion.' He beckoned to one of the groundsmen. 'Do you want him in the clinic, or back to his own place, Shelley?'

'I'll supervise him in the clinic for an hour or two. Give me two minutes to get some clothes on.'

'That would be a pity,' said the lifeguard, in Spanish.

'I heard that,' she told him in the same language. He gave her a bold smile as she turned to get her wrap, then he and the groundsman lifted the holidaymaker and carried him across the grass to the medical centre.

The wife had by now comforted the child, and Shelley stopped to reassure her. 'Sunstroke is the likeliest diagnosis, but I believe in taking great care not to jump to conclusions. I'll monitor him carefully until I'm sure there's nothing else wrong, then you can take him back to your villa.'

'You're very kind, Nurse. We were silly to take so much sun on our first day, but it was just too nice to go in.'

'It's easily done.' Shelley followed the patient up, resigned to missing the seafood dinner she had planned with Rosie. But Rosie wouldn't be alone — she came here every year to run the chemist's shop her father owned, and wasn't likely to be without companionship for the evening.

Shelley was surprised to find her chief in the medical centre. He had been writing at the big desk, and had come round it to examine the patient. She paused in the doorway, and said, 'Shall I take over, Doctor?'

'Thank you, yes. I have some paperwork to finish. Is this just a case of too much sun?'

'I think so, but I'll stay with him for a while, and just give him fluids.'

He nodded, impassive, and went back to his desk. Shelley checked the patient's heart and lungs. He had regained consciousness, but was drowsy and uncomfortable. His blood-pressure was normal, but she found his temperature was raised. She questioned him, trying to find out if he had an infection that could account for the temperature. 'No sore throat? Earache? Any history of waterworks trouble?'

'No. But I had some pain passing water today.'

'I'd better test it.' And a sample tested revealed some inflammation. 'You do seem to have an infection, Mr Kennedy. I think I'd better give you a course of broad-spectrum antibiotics. I'm afraid you'll have to go easy on the Sangria while taking the tablets, and on the swimming too.'

'And the sunbathing!' said the patient ruefully. 'But thank you, Nurse, you've been very kind.'

After Mr Kennedy had been taken back to their villa by his wife, Shelley entered the details of the case into a file, and wondered if she need take any further action. She had told him to come back to see her in a week. But perhaps she ought to have made sure she told him to see his own doctor as soon as he got home? She made a note to that effect.

Time had gone quickly, and she hadn't even noticed when Dr Rafaelo had left. Shelley switched off the lights, and locked the medical room. The evening was lovely, the air warm, transparent and luminous, and the lights of the complex made the white walls of the villas glow, set off against the tall graceful cypresses. She walked slowly down the path that led to the pool, where there was a nightly barbecue under the stars. A woman was singing popular songs, and the holiday-makers were drinking and laughing as they ate their steaks.

A quiet voice behind her made her spin round. 'You are going to eat here?' It was Dr Rafaelo.

'I'm not really very hungry,' she answered. 'I

thought of walking down to the beach and having a hamburger at Pepe's.'

'You have been to Pepe's last Saturday?'

'Yes.'

'And what did you think of the music?'

She smiled. 'It got better after twelve o'clock.'

Her chief's voice was rather superior, as though such enthusiasm were a bit childish. 'Oh, that troubadour fellow, you mean? I can't see what women see in him.'

Shelley looked up at her stolid employer and wished he would unbend just a little. 'Then, Dr Rafaelo, you must be very out of touch.'

'You liked him, then?' Dr Rafaelo sounded bored.

'Very much, Doctor, very much indeed.' And her voice was rather warmer than she intended.

CHAPTER TWO

DURING her first, testing week, Shelley noticed that Dr Rafaelo often turned up while she was working during her morning clinics. At first she felt slightly awkward, but he said little, merely stood and watched her, and she was relieved that she had no difficult cases, but found the work straightforward. He didn't ask her to go to the village surgery, but made it clear that she wasn't to stray too far from the complex when he wasn't there. 'It's easy work,' she confided in Rosie, 'because really I love being here on the complex. There's plenty to do.'

'Yes, I can see you're getting quite pally with Carlos, the friendly lifeguard!'

'He's good fun, and he plays a decent game of tennis. In fact, he said he'd like to come to Pepe's with us on Saturday. Do you mind?'

Rosie said, 'Er—um——' and Shelley guessed that she had other plans for Saturday. She was quite right. 'I've known Francisco for years—I met him the first year I came here, when Monte Samana was brand new.'

'And you have a date for Saturday?'

'Actually, yes. We have a rather special restaurant just outside town—a place where the Spaniards go to eat, not the tourists. It isn't fancy or anything, but the food is great. I'll take you one day. We may join you at Pepe's later on, though.'

'No problem. I'll go to Pepe's with Carlos. As long as I don't miss seeing my beautiful Miguel.'

Rosie tried to warn her. 'Don't try and follow him or anything. Pepe has some bouncers who sort of protect Miguel from his fans.'

'Honestly? Then perhaps he really is someone famous. Has anyone tried to put the lights up when he's singing?'

'Don't even think of it, Shelley. The light switches are behind the bar, and no one can get at them but Pepe himself.'

Shelley smiled. 'Then I'll be content just admiring him. But this time I'll get as near to the front as possible!'

'Much wiser,' said Rosie. 'After all, why try and spoil the mystery? Once you know his real name, would it make any of us any happier?'

'You're quite right, Rosie. He's one of the star attractions of Samana. I'll just go along to admire, like everyone else. That is, if my dear boss doesn't find me something to do on Saturday. He might, you know. I've noticed he pops up when I'm not expecting him.'

They were sitting in one of the cafés eating delicious Knickerbocker Glories after a dinner of pizza and salad. It was very dark tonight, some of the stars hidden by cloud, but it was very hot. Rosie asked, 'Do you like him, Shelley? Your good-looking boss?'

'Why do you ask? He's OK.'

Rosie grinned. 'It's just that he isn't married, you know. Most women go for it as soon as they hear that he's a bachelor. The last three assistants he's had like you all found him very eligible. Set their caps at him, and scared him off.'

'Hmm, I suppose he's eligible all right. I won't be setting any caps at him, I promise you. He's far too boring, when you compare him with someone dishy like Miguel!' But as the promised storm broke, and they sheltered in the café eating more ice-creams, Shelley spent the time trying to imagine anyone setting their cap at her silent and uncommunicative boss.

Late on Friday afternoon Shelley was trying not to think of the exciting young Miguelito, while she was seeing a family of four children who had all caught chickenpox. She was busy trying to explain to the mother that they must be kept in isolation for the rest of their holidays. 'In your case, Mrs Allen, I'd take them home and claim your money back from your insurance.'

'But they aren't really ill, Sister! Just a spot or two, and they're running round quite happily. Are you sure it's chickenpox?'

'Yes, I'm quite sure. And someone else might catch it and get much more than a spot or two, so you see, you must be public-spirited about this. I'm afraid Monte Samana does have rules about this sort of thing.'

After the afflicted family had left, it was almost six, and Shelley went to talk to Victoria, the beautiful Spanish receptionist. 'That was difficult,' sighed Shelley. Victoria had been listening. 'The mother didn't want to lose her holiday.'

Victoria agreed. 'You handled her very well. And of course, she gets her money back, so she can look forward to coming again.' She was locking her desk. Shelley wrote up the case and put the files away. Victoria said, 'You find working with Miguel pleasant?'

Shelley looked up, startled to hear the name. 'Miguel?' Then she laughed. 'Oh, the chief, you mean. Yes, he's all right, I suppose. I thought you meant *the* Miguel—the handsome singer down at Pepe's.'

'You like him better?'

'Oh, I love him! So dashing and debonair. I suppose it's only an act, but he's very good at it.'

Victoria looked pleased. She said, 'So you are not looking at Dr Rafaelo as a potential boyfriend?'

'Good heavens, no.'

'That is good.'

Sensing a note of personal involvement, Shelley said, 'You like him, don't you?'

'I — think I try to protect him.'

'I see. Rosie told me the other nurses who worked here have tried to be more than just assistants to him.'

'That is right. But you — you are not interested in him in that way?'

'Victoria, if it will put your mind at ease, I can assure you that Miguel Rafaelo is about as interesting to me as — as a wardrobe, or a desk — useful, but definitely lacking charisma.'

'That is good.'

'You're welcome to him!' Shelley called, as Victoria walked daintily to the door. '*Buenas noches*, Victoria. Have a nice evening.'

'*Buenas noches*, and enjoy your Saturday at Pepe's!'

'No problem.' Shelley cheerfully closed the drawer of the filing cabinet, put the chair tidily under the desk, and the stethoscope in the cupboard with the instruments. She took one last look around, making sure it was all tidy, before going to the door. But in the doorway blocking her exit stood Dr Miguel Rafaelo, and her heart sank. He had work for her?

But he just wanted to chat. 'Your first week, you enjoyed it?'

'Yes. What did you think of my work?'

'I'm — pleased.' Typical Dr Rafaelo — just pleased, in that quiet, boring voice. No great compliments, no thanks. Just pleased. Then he said, 'How about a drink by the pool?'

'All right.' She was in no hurry, and had made no plans to meet Rosie, since Francisco had come on the scene. She didn't mind talking to the doctor for a few minutes, if that was what he wanted.

He was wearing light trousers today, and a light blue polo shirt that hugged his figure, revealing the muscles of his torso in precise detail. Shelley had to admit that he was a fine example of good health, with a light supple walk, bright clear eyes, a thrusting lean jaw and chin, and not an ounce of fat to spoil the contours of that shirt. Tonight for the first time she saw him as an attractive young man rather than as a boss. But she couldn't forget, as the lights twinkled on around the entire hillside, that this man owned them all, every last apartment, every cypress, every swimming-pool and tennis court. Attractive he might be to some people, but he was out of her league and anyway, she wasn't interested. She would be satisfied with her fantasy man, Miguel the guitar player.

Dr Rafaelo took her down to the poolside. The swimmers and sunbathers had all gone, getting ready for dinner, and the groundsmen were setting up the tables and lighting the barbecue. Blue smoke wreathed upwards into the dark sky. The woman who sang wandered over, carrying her sheets of music, and stopped to say a few words to Dr Rafaelo before going up to the little stage and setting up her recording deck to accompany her nightly concert.

'Señor Rafaelo, this is an honour.' The head waiter came over to them. 'Señorita Shelley, good evening. I hope you will stay for the barbecue. We have a good beef tonight.'

Shelley started to reply, but her chief spoke more loudly, drowning her refusal. 'Yes, we'll eat here tonight, won't we, Shelley?' It was the first time he had used her name, and it sounded nice in his slightly accented English.

'If you say so.'

'Shelley, you don't sound very keen. Is it that you prefer not to have to eat dinner with a wardrobe?'

Abashed, realising that he had overheard her conversation with Victoria, Shelley didn't try to make excuses. Instead she smiled, and said, 'Well, I'm sure you're a very nice wardrobe, Doctor. And don't forget, we don't know each other very well yet. You probably think the same of me.'

'In fact, I'm impressed with you. The way you dealt with that man who collapsed was exemplary. I like the way you deal with people. And I like your obvious sympathy with my people in Santa Barbara village.'

'Well, thank you.'

'As you know, I am a man of few words. I don't go over the top with compliments. So all I ask is that you go on the way you have started.'

'No problem.' She was looking at him now, wishing he would unbend a little more, maybe sit back and enjoy the evening, and allow his sleeked-back hair to fall more naturally about his face. With a little more animation, he could pass for a really handsome man. She began to see why the previous nurses had all thought him worth chasing after.

'Do you remember I asked you a question on your first day that you refused to answer?' he said. 'About your previous job? You were a top-grade sister, yet you threw it all away to take a non-challenging temporary post here for half a year. Why? There has to be a reason.'

The waiter had brought a jug of wine and two glasses, and Miguel poured out the sparkling liquid. They both drank, conscious that it had been a long afternoon, and Shelley at least was thirsty. When she put the glass down, she saw that he was still waiting for a reply. 'I can always take up my career again if I go back. My qualifications won't go away.'

'If you go back? Not when?'

'Exactly, Doctor. If. I didn't want to grow old having never had any excitement in my life. My parents are both dead, and I've worked since I left school, at one thing and another. My career always came first. I suddenly decided I wanted to see and do something different.'

'I'm glad you chose Samana,' he told her gravely. 'And I think it will be a long time before you grow old, Shelley.'

There was something in his voice that suddenly got

through to her, and she felt a little tendril of pleasure unwinding inside. 'Thank you.'

'Have you found any excitement yet?'

She smiled at that. 'You overheard what I was saying to Victoria, didn't you, Doctor? I don't know how much you heard, but I liked the music at Pepe's last Saturday. I do hope there won't be any emergencies to keep me from going again tomorrow.'

'Or if there is an emergency, you want me to deal with it while you go and swoon over that dandy Miguel?'

She ignored his condescending tone, and said, 'Yes, frankly, that is what I hope.'

'Shelley, as I said before, you are very outspoken. But of course, you aren't out to trap me into matrimony, so it is easier for you to be frank. I find it a refreshing change. Would you like me to order you a steak? How do you like yours done?'

He had changed the subject too quickly for her to answer him, so she didn't bother trying. After all, it was true. She didn't want her relationship with her chief to become any closer than it was at present. All the same, it was flattering to be chosen to spend the evening with him, and she could see that he was visibly beginning to relax with her, which was nice — a sort of compliment.

'Why are you smiling?' he asked. They were dealing with the steaks, which fulfilled the savoury promise that filled the air around the big stone barbecue and tasted delicious. He poured more wine.

She said lightly, 'Because you are looking more at ease with me. Don't worry, I know why. I'm the comfortable type, not the glamorous type.'

'The feminine equivalent of a wardrobe?'

She laughed aloud and agreed with him. 'Exactly, Doctor.'

'I wish you would call me Miguel.'

'All right. There's no danger of mixing you up with the mystery man from Pepe's.'

'I should hope not.'

'Can you sing, Miguel?'

'I suppose so, in the bath.'

'I find the Spanish terribly emotional where music is concerned. It's so — explicit, and natural. I find it very exciting.'

'So music is the one thing that weakens your British reserve, Shelley?'

'Music if it's Miguelito's. He sings with such genuine feeling.'

'It's all an act, my dear. Don't let him take you in. It's designed for greatest impact on gullible female tourists.'

She laughed. 'Well, it works, so don't sound so superior! That handsome young man is helping to bring visitors back to your holiday complex to make more money for you!'

'I suppose he is.' Miguel Rafaelo didn't seem to have thought of that. 'Well, I won't criticise his brash style, then.'

'Brash? How could you? He's dashing — swashbuckling — and so terrific-looking!'

'Camp! Artificial! Commercial!'

The wine had made her talkative, and she said quite naturally, 'Oh, there's no arguing with you. You don't understand! I say, Miguel, you're quite an important chap around here. Do you think you could ask Pepe if I could meet him? Surely you of all people could say the word?'

Their plates were cleared away, and Rafaelo snapped his fingers for more wine. The singer was ready to start, and some couples were already dancing to her tapes. 'I suppose I could arrange an introduction, if that's what you really want. But I think it would spoil everything for you, when you realise he's just a boring, pushy young fellow with an ego the size of the bullring.'

Shelley smiled at him and wagged her finger. 'Do I detect a tiny note of jealousy? You could be fun too, you know, if you'd only unbend a little. But I suppose tycoons don't unbend. It wouldn't be proper.'

He smiled back, and held out one hand to her. 'Dance with me?'

'Oh.' She came down to earth then. Some couples were dancing, and the moon was bright, the atmosphere definitely romantic. Something began to scare her, as he repeated his invitation to dance. She didn't want to get any closer. She didn't really want him to touch her. . .'That was the wine talking, not Shelley Cameron. And I couldn't possibly dance wearing uniform. Don't forget, we only came down here for a drink. If I'd known it was dinner, I'd have changed into something more suitable.'

'If I'd told you it was dinner you would have made an excuse.'

'I wouldn't!'

'You would.'

'Prove it.'

'I don't have to. Your own words proved it, when you were talking to Victoria about me.'

'Oh.' Shelley smiled at him. She felt she had been rather too brutally frank, and regretted it, because she didn't dislike Miguel Rafaelo. 'Miguel, I apologise if I said anything unflattering about you. I've enjoyed tonight with you very much. But I think after three glasses of wine it's time I went home.'

'I understand. Let me walk up with you. You have one of the villas on the high point of the hill, don't you?'

'Yes—Rosie's parents own it. It has a wonderful view. I adore it in the early mornings, when the sun is still behind the hill. And in the evenings, when the afterglow makes the whole valley magic.'

He looked at her then in a strange and thoughtful way, and she felt it was with approval. His voice was gentle. 'I know what you mean.' He didn't touch her as they walked casually up the winding road to the high point. 'In a way, it could be said I've ruined the valley by putting up these houses,' he said. 'But I like to think that if I didn't do it, someone else would have done it with a lot less taste and love for the countryside.'

Shelley agreed. 'And you look after the villagers too. I saw the way you had all the time in the world to chat to the patients in Santa Barbara, and help them without charging anything. You must be an understanding, kindly sort of person, Miguel, behind your rather forbidding manner.'

'Forbidding? Me? Is that what you think?'

They had stopped on the high point, where they could look across their own little valley to the dark sea, and back into another valley lined with lush woods. The stars lit up the scene, and the little black iron lamps that gleamed outside each villa, in perfect keeping with the traditional style of the architecture. Down beneath them the lights round the swimming-pool shone cheerfully, and the voice of the singer floated up to them in the starlight, as in a natural amphitheatre. Crickets were singing loudly up here, and a gentle breeze stirred the leaves of the cypresses.

Shelley heard his footstep in the grass as he turned to face her, and slowly took off his glasses and pushed them into his back pocket; but she wasn't prepared for being taken bodily into his arms and soundly kissed. He was very strong, and she was too surprised to protest or struggle anyway, and stood with his hand supporting her head, as his warm lips pressed against hers, and his warm tongue flickered between them.

She hadn't expected this. One minute they were having a philosophical discussion, and the next a very physical encounter, in which Shelley felt that her companion had the greater advantage. He had clearly done this before. Shelley hadn't, much, and her first impression, after her shock, was fear. What if he didn't stop? What if he tried to overpower her? But slowly her body began to respond to the powerful but gentle kisses, and she began to lose her apprehension. It was, after all, a wonderful sensation creeping through her in response to his lips, and she found herself drifting into co-operation with him, holding his perfect body against her, feeling his heart beat and knowing that they fitted together in a most satisfactory way.

Finally he raised his head and whispered, 'Goodnight, Shelley.'

She found herself at a loss for words. Slowly she began to come back to reality, and realise that she had been entirely at his mercy. Her fear came back, and with it, anger. 'You—shouldn't have done that!'

'Didn't you like it? I thought you did, all in all.'

'No, I didn't like it. I—was taken by surprise. And I hadn't given my permission.'

'You would have said no,' he whispered, 'and I didn't want to be refused.'

'Of course I would have refused. I don't see you—like that, in that way. You're my employer, that's all. You really had no right to—to—shock me that way!'

His voice was very smooth. 'But you have enjoyed the evening?'

'Yes—until now.'

Miguel took her chin in his hand and tipped her face up towards him. He looked less threatening when she could see the sincerity in his eyes, and his hair, finally loosened from its severe style, waving naturally round his ears. 'Forgive me, Shelley. I didn't realise.'

'Didn't realise what?'

'Your virginity, your fear. It won't happen again. Maybe you should have told me more about what made you leave your hospital? There was a man there, wasn't there? Someone you had feelings for?'

'There's no need to talk about it.'

Dr Rafaelo moved his hand from her face, and she felt a sense of loss, wanting its warmth back again. He said, 'Goodnight, *señorita*. Perhaps it is better that you are with a wardrobe. I believe if you had that Mystery Miguel here instead of me, he would not have understood your feelings. He would have taken what he wanted, Shelley. He's that sort of man. He wouldn't understand inhibitions.'

'I don't have inhibitions.' But she didn't say it with any conviction. And Dr Rafaelo was the kind of man she felt she could talk to openly. 'Oh — maybe I do. Maybe I liked the Mystery Man because he represents no threat — he would never have time for someone as ordinary as me.'

Dr Rafaelo smiled, as he took his glasses out and put them on again, and smoothed his hair back. 'One thing I must remember to teach you while you are working for me, Shelley, is not to be afraid to be beautiful. But I think perhaps you have had enough lessons for one night. Sleep well, my little friend. I'll see you on Monday. Enjoy your weekend. I hope you see your Miguelito.'

She watched him find his way deftly down the hill towards the tiny rectangle of blue that was the swimming-pool. She heard him even after she had lost sight of him, those sure footsteps crunching on the stones. She stood for a long time, trying to make sense of her feelings, the words he had said tumbling around in her brain.

He was nice, but he was more dangerous than she had thought. There must be no more cosy dinners for two. She might, heaven forbid, allow herself to fall for him, and suffer the fate of the last three nurses whom he had rejected, according to Victoria, after they had expected more from him than just mild flirtation. Well, that wouldn't happen with Shelley Cameron.

'Inhibitions, indeed!' She didn't know whether to be

pleased or angry. But her thoughts were brought to an abrupt end, as she descried two figures on their way up the path, and knew she must vacate the viewpoint for Rosie and her Francisco. It must be nice to have an uncomplicated relationship.

It was a foursome in Pepe's on Saturday, and Shelley let her hair down in more ways than one, dancing vigorously with the hunky Carlos, while Rosie and her good-looking little Francisco sat in the shadows, their heads close together. In fact time went so quickly that Shelley was surprised when the crowded room fell silent, and the sound of the church clock in the square drifted through the little café. Then Shelley felt a shiver of anticipation, as she remembered the effect the first sight of the handsome Miguelito had on her.

She felt herself moving to the side with the others, as the lights were lowered, and a stool placed in the centre of the dance-floor. The last chime quivered away on the night air, and from somewhere behind the bar emerged the local hero, Miguelito the mystery man. Yes, he was as charismatic as she remembered, with his wide smile, his open greeting as he kissed his hand to all the girls, and bowed low, so that his curls fell over his face, and had to be swept back with a gesture that was both appealing and very sexy. Someone threw a bunch of red roses, which he caught and put on the bar. He was wearing a white shirt tonight, with very full sleeves and ruffles down the front. His legs were encased in tight black trousers that outlined his figure tantalisingly; the light was not quite bright enough to see his full silhouette.

Shelley gazed as he sang, wondering if Dr Rafaelo had been right in saying that this act was only showmanship, with no genuine feeling or emotion in it. She couldn't agree. Miguelito sang with a tremulous intensity, and his guitar playing was light, passionate and extremely skilful. Why else did the locals love him as much as the visitors?

She tried to elbow her way closer to the front. If only the lights were brighter. Why didn't they use a spotlight? Was he really a famous opera star? Or perhaps he was older than he looked, and didn't want his fans to know it? But no, by his very movement it was plain that he was supple and vigorous, full of life and passion and promise. She did want to meet him, talk with him, find out if his mind was as beautiful as his body and his talent. But as soon as he launched into the dance music, the local girls clattered in, shaking their skirts, their handsome heads held high, rosy lips and black eyes catching the light, and shielding the guitar player from his audience.

But tonight, after the dancing and the cheers, Miguelito didn't just slip away. Instead he took a curtain call, and at the last minute before he was to slide behind the curtains behind the bar, he reached for the flowers thrown to him earlier and broke off some of the roses, swaggering round the circle of admirers handing out the roses to the women. Shelley, at the front, felt herself growing hot as he approached. Would she receive a rose from these talented hands? He was nearing her, his face almost invisible because the light was behind him. She could only see the glint of the whites of his eyes, and the gleam of his teeth as he smiled at her. '*Señorita!*' She could feel the warmth of his breath on her cheek as the rose was pressed into her hand.

And then he was gone, and the fans were left cheering his showmanship, while the girls who had roses held them as though they were made of gold. Rosie said, 'So you're one of the favoured, Shelley!'

They returned to their seats, where Carlos had bought iced colas for them all. Shelley came out of her dream, and tried to play down her starstruck behaviour. 'Well, it's all part of the act,' she said, shrugging her shoulders. But she smelt the rose, and felt very happy.

'But I bet you keep that rose forever,' said Carlos, laughing. 'What chance for ordinary boys with that joker around!'

And then Pepe himself came over to their table. 'You are Señorita Cameron? I have a message from the Monte Samana. Someone is ill, and is asking for help. The doctor is busy, and told me to tell you to go.'

Shelley stood up at once. 'Of course. You don't know what illness the patient has? I'll go at once. No need for anyone else to break up the party.'

Carlos said, 'I will come, Shelley. You need a lift — and anyway, why should I stay without my partner to dance with?'

She refused to let him. 'Because there are lots of pretty girls around, Carlos. Don't you dare miss out on the fun.' She picked up her rose on her way out.

She came out into the starlit night, and beckoned one of the battered taxis to take her the short distance to the Monte Samana complex. The guard on the gate recognised her, and saluted as the taxi swung in. She ran to the medical centre, where the door was open and the light on. Dr Rafaelo was standing with his arms folded across his chest, and a very bad-tempered look on his face. Shelley went in. 'What happened?' she asked. I thought there was an emergency.

'No emergency — just a drunken spree. I'm sorry, Shelley — this must have spoiled your evening. I've sent the boy away with his friends. They made him drink too much. They can look after him.'

She fingered the rose in her hands and said, 'You don't think he ought to be supervised? Some of these young boys can be quite ill. . .'

'Give me credit for knowing an illness when I see it, Shelley.' He came towards her and put his hand on her shoulder. 'Thank you for coming so quickly. Sorry to waste your time.'

'It doesn't matter. I'm ready for bed anyway.'

'I see you have a rose — a sign of love. It's beautiful. Who gave you that?'

She smiled. 'It's a secret.'

With his gentlest voice he said, 'Not really. Your Miguelito. Perhaps you really will attract his attention if you go on like this. Then you'll be begging me to look after you.'

'That's not really likely, Miguel. But — will you? Look after me?'

'You can trust me, *señorita*.' They exchanged a long look as they both thought of the kisses they had shared, and Shelley's furious rebuke. 'Shall I walk you home tonight?'

She looked down at the rose. Somehow she didn't want to spoil the lovely feeling of being close to Miguelito, hearing his romantic whisper, '*Señorita*...'

'No, thank you. I'll be fine.' She wished him goodnight, and set off to walk up the hill, her feet scarcely touching the ground. She didn't notice Miguel Rafaelo watching her until her slight form merged into the darkness. There was a satisfied smile on his handsome face.

CHAPTER THREE

VICTORIA was apparently becoming concerned. 'You see too much of the doctor, Shelley.'

'Nonsense. Don't blame me, Victoria. I only work for him.'

'I know that. But, Shelley, the idea was for you to work here at Monte Samana while he works at Santa Barbara. More and more you seem to me to be going together to the village.'

'I can't help that. He's the boss, remember. I don't ask to go. I'd much rather sit by the pool.'

'You are encouraging him.' The pretty Spaniard appeared to be genuinely upset. 'I've seen those sideways glances. You have very pretty eyes, you know, Shelley. He has noticed.'

'What sideways glances? Victoria, I've told you already, he appeals to me about as much as a piece of furniture. He's just there. You don't have to worry—I won't forget your warning about all the other nurses who've worked for him here. I promise not to fall for your boss, Victoria, OK? There's no need to protect him from me. I don't see him in that way at all.'

'Are you really sure about that? Sometimes a person can fall in love without realising it.' The young woman seemed to know what she was talking about, and Shelley suddenly felt sorry for her, in spite of her flashing Spanish beauty.

Shelley was putting her drawer of patients' notes in alphabetical order, but she looked up from her work to ask quietly, 'Do you care for Dr Rafaelo?'

Victoria was disconcerted by the question. 'As a friend, yes.'

Shelley decided to tease her a little. 'Well, that's all

he is to me, I promise. I know I couldn't fall in love without knowing it. My feet are firmly on the ground. Anyway, I'm only being friendly with Dr Rafaelo so that he'll arrange a meeting for me with the handsome Miguelito. Now there is a man I could fall for.'

'I know.' Victoria laughed suddenly. 'I saw the rose he gave you at the back of the drawer, wrapped in silver foil!'

Shelley fell silent. She had kept the rose, naturally. Who wouldn't? But she recalled Dr Rafaelo's words, that Miguelito wasn't the sort of person to respect a girl's feelings. 'He would have taken what he wanted.' Did she really want to believe herself in love with a man like that? And she knew she didn't. All the same, every Saturday was the same, that thrill of excitement as the clock struck midnight, and her own breathless hope as Miguelito's lively black eyes roved the audience, and sometimes rested on her as his liquid voice accompanied his virtuoso guitar playing. . .

She said thoughtfully, 'I suppose I'm just gullible, allowing a man's sheer showmanship to affect me like that.'

Victoria laughed and said, 'You are in good company, Shelley. He is as popular with the local girls as with the visitors. He has genuine talent.'

'It's more than that, Victoria. He has charisma coming out of his ears. Even before he plays a note, he has the audience in the palm of his hand. I suppose, like all the rest, I'm just in love with a figment of my own imagination. That's what having heroes is all about. Get to know them, and they're never as glamorous or as perfect as one imagines.'

A masculine voice joined in the conversation, and they turned to see Dr Rafaelo at the door, with a broad smile on his face. His hair was severely brushed back, but his eyes were lively behind the thick-rimmed glasses. 'Well, how very lucky I am to have an assistant with her feet planted so very firmly on the ground! I take it you girls are discussing the Samana singing idol again?'

Shelley replied, because Victoria was merely smiling and shaking her cloud of dark hair. She was annoyed with herself for allowing this man to overhear her secret thoughts. 'Dr Rafaelo, you do have a very bad habit of listening at doors to private conversations.'

'If they're private, don't have them in my consulting-rooms, then.' His voice was offhand, as he strode in and put his neat briefcase down on the desk. 'I'll take over here, if you two want a break.'

Victoria was off at once. 'Thank you, Miguel. I did want to go to the boutique. They are getting some new designs in this morning, and I must see them before they are snapped up.'

As the door swung to behind her, Dr Rafaelo said, 'And you, Shelley? Don't you want to see the new designs?'

'No way, thank you. I couldn't afford them even if I liked anything.'

'They will keep it for you, you know — you can pay by instalments.'

She scolded him then, in her cheerful way that she knew he didn't mind. 'Miguel, don't you be making me spend my money if I don't want to! I'm no tycoon, you know!' And as he held his finger to his lips, she remembered that he had told her in strict confidence that the complex belonged to him. 'I'm sorry. I didn't mean to say that. I promise I've told no one else.'

'That's all right, Shelley. But there's a forfeit to pay for forgetting my confidence — will you have dinner with me tonight?'

She liked her boss a lot more now than she had at the beginning of their relationship. But she had made up her mind never to allow herself to get close to him, in case there was a repetition of that first rather disturbing kiss. So she said, 'No, Miguel, if it's all the same to you. I'd rather keep our — friendship — strictly businesslike.'

His slow smile lit up his eyes, and again she realised with a jolt that behind his severe exterior he could be quite attractive. He said, 'There you are, you see — never accepting any invitations. You're scared, Shelley — scared of yourself.'

'No, I'm not,' she denied.

'I said I would have to teach you to be beautiful, and I don't intend to fail.'

'Don't hold your breath, Miguel, because I'm not going out with you.'

'Not even to Pepe's?'

Shelley paused, her mouth already opening to refuse. 'Pepe's? On Saturday?'

He was smiling broadly now. 'You see? I hold a trump card! I could introduce you to Miguelito.'

She decided he was only teasing her. 'Och, you're kidding. I don't believe you. Anyway, I've changed my mind — you heard me talking to Victoria before — I don't want to meet him! I don't want my illusions shattered.'

Miguel Rafaelo said quietly, 'You don't want to come face to face with yourself, then, Shelley. One day you're going to have to face it, either by telling me, or telling someone. Who was it who drove you inside yourself at that big hospital in England? Who upset you so much that you are afraid now of being beautiful in case you get hurt again?'

His voice was very gentle, and she knew she could trust him. Perhaps he was right. Ken Noakes had been a brute to her, thoughtlessly and selfishly, and she realised it now. She said curiously, 'Miguel, tell me the truth. Am I even a little bit — beautiful, or are you just saying it to make me open up?'

He didn't move closer to her, but his voice was little more than a whisper. Somehow at that moment he was very far from being just part of the furniture. His words, in that elusively caressing accent, floated to her in the quiet little office. 'You are a very lovely woman. You have a face like a perfect marble statue, yet I know you are not stone inside. I know it, and I have only kissed you once.'

He took one step closer. She felt his hands on her shoulders, and knew that any minute now the grip would tighten, and she would find herself in his arms. She couldn't move. Yet she still had the use of her tongue, and she said as quietly as he, 'Yes, only once — and let's keep it like that, shall we?'

'Shelley,' he purred, 'how could we?' And she felt the puff of his warm breath on her cheek before she felt the softness of his lips on her mouth. Like last time, she stood, captivated by his unthreatening embrace, warmed and stirred by his gentle yet potentially passionate kisses. It was definitely a prelude to more, and she knew she must start to struggle soon. Very soon. . . Instead, her arms crept round his body, and her hands spread over his back, as she felt his muscles straining to hold her closer. The shape of his spine seemed to ask to be stroked, and his sharp intake of breath when she did so made her more aware suddenly of her own power to affect him. Dare to be beautiful. . . Dared she? Or not yet?

A sudden sharp ring at the doorbell made Shelley's decision for her, as they sprang apart, and she smoothed her uniform down and went to the reception desk to see who wanted her. She recognised Rosie's Francisco. 'Hi, what can I do for you, Francisco?' she said, hoping he didn't notice her pink cheeks and slightly flurried manner.

He didn't, because he was holding a towel over his hand, and the towel was turning a bright red even as he stood. Francisco worked in Admin, but occasionally he doubled as a barman, and he didn't have to explain that he had cut himself on a broken glass. Miguel Rafaelo was there beside them, exuding calm and confidence. 'I'll hold the tourniquet while you get the needle and silk.' Shelley was already reaching for the suturing packs. She poured the antiseptic liquid into a bowl, and gently unwrapped the towel while Rafaelo kept pressure on the vein to stop the bleeding. He murmured, 'Try to clean the area for me, Shelley.'

She wiped enough blood away for them to see that it was a clean cut, the edges easy for Miguel's skilful fingers to pull together. As he did the actual stitching, Shelley took over the grip on the tourniquet, until the skin was pulled together, and she was able to give the whole area a good wipe of iodine, before putting a clean dry dressing on the hand. 'You won't be going back to work for a few days, I'm afraid, Francisco.'

'Lucky for me you were both here.'

Miguel Rafaelo smiled slightly. 'You're right, Francisco—very lucky. I'm due at the village, only Shelley kept me—talking.' And his smile made Shelley blush again, although this time she wasn't as angry as last time with him for kissing her. Now why was that? Surely he was still as dangerous? Surely she was still as determined as ever not to allow anyone to creep through her defences and make her care? Surely she didn't want to be number four?

She said stoutly, 'Shall I walk back with you, Francisco?'

'I am all right, thank you, Shelley. I will make the most of being injured, and go down and sit by the pool for a while and chat to Carlos.'

They watched him stroll down and seat himself under Carlos's striped umbrella. Dr Rafaelo said, 'Well, Shelley, shall we go to the village surgery now?'

'If you say so. You're the boss. But Victoria is wondering why I always come with you, when I was employed to be on duty here.'

His voice was cool and unemotional, as he went through to pick up his medical case. 'You should have told her that we like to work together.' He looked up and caught her staring at him. He smiled very slightly. 'Don't we?'

He was right, but she wasn't going to admit it. She had to fight to keep away from him. 'Not really. I'm happier working alone, not having my work judged all the time.'

'Rubbish. You already know that I admire your work. You are not being judged—you are being admired.'

'And that is part of your therapy for poor frigid Shelley, is that it?' Her voice rose, as she thought she realised why he had kissed her earlier. 'Well, Miguel, you can leave me out of your rehabilitation programme, thank you. I'm no guinea-pig. You might mean well, but find someone else to experiment on!'

'Stop talking, Shelley, and get into the jeep.'

She appealed to him then. 'Can't I stay here this time?'

His attitude was casual. 'Naturally, if you wish. But you did want to see how little Cara's leg is healing, didn't you? And you did tell old Grandfather Freitas that you would see him again about his chest. Giving up the pipe, you remember? You were having more success than I.'

'Oh, yes, you know I do, of course.' And there was nothing to do here. Shelley went outside to the jeep, parked close by in the blazing sun, but turned as Miguel followed her and suggested, 'Maybe I could go to the village alone? There's no need for both of us to go, and you know it.'

'If you like.' He was non-committal, and she was surprised and relieved that he had agreed so swiftly. 'Will you need a medical bag? Here, take mine.' And he thrust it into the jeep, as Shelley, rather puzzled by his ready agreement, shifted herself into the driving seat. She started the engine. He said no more, so she drove away, without looking back. It was a relief in a way to be alone, without Miguel always so quiet and thoughtful by her side. He disturbed her even when he said nothing, because she knew she couldn't read his mind. It was better to make it clear right from the start that she preferred to work in the other surgery alone, rather than work together in both village and complex.

In the village surgery, there was the usual group of chatting neighbours, who seemed to find themselves so much at home that if Shelley hadn't turned up, they would still have sat there quite happily, passing the time of day. But they greeted her as an old friend. *'Enfermera Señorita Shelley! Buenos días. Cómo está usted?'*

She laughed and tried out her Spanish. *'Muy buena, gracias.'*

'Where is Dr Miguel?'

'Not coming today. Do you wish to see him?'

'Oh no, no. You are just as good. And you are easier on the eye.'

Shelley took the compliments as they were meant, kindly. 'Now, let me see you, Abuelo Freitas.' Everybody called him Grandfather. She had never heard anyone call him anything else but Abuelo. 'How is your cough?'

'Very bad, Nurse Shelley. It was better with the pipe.'

'That's what I expected you to say. But you want to live to see your fifth grandchild, I think? So keep it up.'

'But Lina is only four months with child.'

'Good. Then by the time he's born, you'll be a new man, isn't that right?'

When she had seen all the ailments, Shelley stayed to talk. They were anxious to tell her about Miguel Rafaelo, whom they obviously loved. 'He is one of us. He lives here on that hill behind the village. Can you see the villa, set among the vineyards?' It looked simple, a low white building with a shady arcade around it, and a couple of cars parked to one side.

Shelley stared at a carved gateway painted white and blue, with two large blue plantpots outside, and two palm trees inside. She imagined the young doctor coming to this simple village, the home of his grandmother, to build his business empire, getting to know and love the villagers as he did so, and deciding to live with them and spend his spare time caring for them as a doctor.

'He lives alone?'

Abuelo Freitas cackled. 'Oh, yes — how else should a bachelor live? He doesn't want his mother along, especially when he brings young Victoria to visit.'

'Victoria? His receptionist?'

'That is what he calls her!'

'Does she come often?'

'Sure, they eat in the café here many times.'

It made sense, Shelley decided. Victoria was an extremely pretty young woman, and it was obvious that she cared for Miguel Rafaelo. She would make a good wife, when he decided to settle down. No wonder she made it clear to Shelley that she was wasting her time. Shelley left the village, after sharing a jug of wine with the Freitas family, and promising to come again soon. She made a deliberate detour past Miguel's house on her way back to Monte Samana, and, without stopping, noted that it was called Casa Madrid. She was tempted to stop and pry, but common sense reminded her that she wasn't interested in Dr Miguel Rafaelo, and it would do no good to show curiosity.

When she got back, Miguel was still in the medical centre, chatting to Victoria. Shelley returned the medical bag, and would have left them together, but Miguel called her back. 'Have you been to the cove yet, Shelley?'

'No. Rosie promised to take me on her next day off.'

'Then I'll take you. Purely business, naturally.'

Shelley said vehemently, 'I don't want to go to the cove. I can swim quite well in the pool if I want to.'

His tone became severe. 'I have to show you what provisions we have for medical emergencies down there—lifelines, resuscitation equipment, that sort of thing. Bring your bathing-suit, just in case—in case anyone looks as though they might be drowning,' he finished, toning down the severity of his voice with one of his enigmatic smiles.

'It makes sense for me to know what you have there, I suppose.' Her voice was brisk. 'I hope you won't think I'm just coming to enjoy myself.'

He said calmly, as he put the jeep into gear, 'You wouldn't know the meaning of the word.'

'I would so! I've enjoyed myself very much so far—with my work.'

'Exactly. And with the mythical Miguelito, whom you admire as long as he doesn't want to touch you.'

'Oh, don't bring him up again. You don't like him because he's better-looking than you!' she accused.

He gave her a sideways glance that was positively superior. 'To be honest, I think I have a better profile.'

'There's no comparison!' Shelley was laughing now, feeling that ease that happened more frequently these days, the ease that came when they were together and became, quite suddenly and pleasantly, totally relaxed with each other.

He drove along a narrow private stony path. 'There is a regular bus service from Monte Samana for the guests, but this is the way the natives come, straight over the hill.' He rounded a sharp bend, and suddenly the deep blue Mediterranean lay there, a secluded cove with an outcrop of dark rocks, and a semi-circular sandy bay.

'Oh, it's lovely,' breathed Shelley. 'And there's a restaurant too!' A winding wooden staircase led to an open-sided wooden shack perched precariously on the rocks, whence came a savoury smell and some aromatic smoke. 'A barbecue!'

Miguel said, 'Fresh-caught fish in olive oil and garlic, with local wine. You refused to accept my offer of dinner, but now that we are here you aren't going to refuse to eat with me?'

She gazed, enchanted, at the little restaurant. It would be silly not to see inside. 'No, I couldn't refuse this. The smell is persuading me.'

'Well said. You're learning.'

'When will you understand that I don't need your teaching? I'm quite happy with myself, thank you.'

He stripped off his shirt and jeans and stood in brief bathing-trunks looking down at her, his tanned legs and muscular body catching the sun. With a casual grin, he said, 'And I'm quite happy with you too, just now.' And he took off his glasses, tucking them into the pile of clothes, and ran down to the edge of the water. As she joined him, rather shyly accepting his glance of approval at her slim body in its white bikini, the wind stirred his hair, blowing it out of its rigidly swept-back style. Shelley felt a tug at her heart at the sudden attraction of him, the perfect body and the face that looked so much more natural and attractive out here in the warm southern wind.

As though he read her mind, Miguel moved closer to her, ignoring the groups of holidaymakers under their sun-loungers, and pulled her against him. The shock of her bare skin against his took her breath away. It was indecent, surely, to stand like this, in public, and feel so alive and so excited? Angry with herself for being so easily led, Shelley pulled away from him and ran headlong into the water, which was colder than she expected, in spite of the hot sun. She dived down and swam out strongly against the current, towards an orange buoy at the outer edge of the bay.

While she swam, she felt safe. Thoughts tumbled about in her brain, thoughts and words and feelings.

She knew now how attractive Miguel could be when he wanted to be, and she knew he could manipulate her feelings. Yet both Rosie and Victoria had warned her against letting herself fall for him, in case she followed the same fate as his other nurses. And also Shelley knew from the villagers that Victoria was a frequent visitor to his villa. She would be totally crazy to allow any further familiarity with Miguel Rafaelo, no matter how attractive he was beginning to appear to her. Shelley Cameron wasn't cheap, and wouldn't have people saying so.

Then suddenly his dark head appeared beside her, and he was swimming strongly beside her. 'Are you thinking of going all the way to Morocco?' he asked, with his even white teeth shining as he smiled and dived down like a dolphin around her.

She stopped swimming and trod water while she looked back. 'I do seem to have come quite a long way.'

'I thought you were trying to get away from me.'

'You wouldn't be far wrong at that.'

'Let's go back.' He reached out and took hold of her hand that was nearest to him in the blue-green water.

'Miguel, when we go back, can I be treated simply as your nurse, your employee? I find it very disturbing and unwelcome to have you go touching me as you do. I don't like it, and it's nothing at all to do with being frigid. It's nothing at all to do with Ken Noakes either. I just don't want to be treated like——'

'Like a woman?'

'Like an object—a toy to be played with. Can you understand that, Miguel?'

'Of course. I understand you loud and clear, and it will be just as you desire, I promise.' He wasn't abashed by her request, and as his gentle gaze roamed over her face, she felt that he did indeed understand her rather too well.

She began to swim back to shore. 'Thanks. Now that we understand one another I feel better. I don't want to be number four in your list of discarded nurses.'

'Number——?' He seemed to realise what she was saying. 'Ah, I see. Discarded nurses. Victoria has been talking, hasn't she? I must have a word with her when we get back.'

'Don't bother. Just forget it, please.' They walked up the beach to where they had left their towels. Shelley noticed that he put his glasses on as soon as he had towelled his face and head dry, and combed back his damp hair. With the glasses he seemed to put on another nature—his stern, cool attitude she had first noted, and felt unthreatened by. 'We'll take a look at the medical supplies. They have to be checked regularly, you understand.'

'Of course.' She rubbed herself as dry as possible, and wrapped a pareo round her waist. 'I'm ready.'

They walked up the steep cliff path and checked the life-saving equipment and the box of emergency supplies. Then Miguel led the way up the rickety staircase to the restaurant, where, at a click of his fingers, they were supplied with a plate of olives and a jug of deep red Sangria.

With grave face and totally businesslike voice he began to talk about the beginnings of this place, of the way he had planned and discussed the enterprise, and how he had enabled the local people to be involved all the way through, so that they knew what he was planning, and they didn't feel threatened by him, but collaborated with him, knowing that it meant jobs, roads and plumbing and a higher standard of living for them all.

Gradually Shelley began to relax. This was a side of him she admired and liked, and as long as they could talk like this she was happy and open to chat, even to tease. She knew she ought not to mind his advances—

they were only natural really, and in a way a compliment. But they spoiled the relationship of employer and employee. Now that he was being the perfect gentleman in not pursuing her, at last she began to breathe more easily. The sun was setting behind the black rocks, and the sea was a blaze of luminous colour. She gazed out as the beach gradually emptied of holidaymakers, and felt grateful to Rosie for having persuaded her to come to Samana.

They drove back to Monte Samana in silence, and Miguel stopped near the medical centre. The sky was studded with stars, and the lilting voice of the folk singer at the barbecue drifted over the floodlit lawns. Couples were dancing, slowly, cheek to cheek, by the pool. Miguel said, 'Goodnight, Shelley.'

'Goodnight.' Suddenly she didn't want to be alone, but she knew she could not say so. It was better this way. She swung herself lightly from the jeep and walked slowly alongside the pool. You are here to work, Shelley Cameron, she told herself. Let's not have any more tomfoolery with your feelings. Thank goodness your boss has turned himself back into a wardrobe...

CHAPTER FOUR

FOR the next few days Shelley didn't catch even a glimpse of her chief. She didn't mention it to Victoria, but by the end of the week she couldn't help being a little curious. There had been very few patients. She had lazed around the pool to her heart's content—and she had played tennis with Carlos three times. Carlos was an easygoing young man, with so many girlfriends that Shelley knew they were only going to be friends, nothing more.

And then Mrs Richards happened. An elderly lady who owned one of the bigger villas, Mrs Richards was a well-known figure on the complex, trotting along to the sauna with her parasol shielding her face from the hot sun, and eating paella regularly at Don Pedro's restaurant before taking a dip in the pool. She walked, that Friday morning, halting and clutching at her chest, into the medical centre, and her face was grey with pain.

Shelley's reaction was instantaneous. 'Oh, Mrs Richards—come in, sit down, please—what a good thing I was here.' She rushed to support the plucky little woman.

'I think it must be my heart.' Mrs Richards had always been succinct. 'It hurts a lot—just here.'

'A chest pain? Come, lie down, let me examine you.' Mrs Richards' pulse was faint, and her features drawn with stress. Shelley listened to her chest, and heard the tell-tale irregular heartbeat, saw the clammy face and grey pallor. 'Mrs Richards, I must call an ambulance.' She turned to Victoria. 'Get hold of Miguel, please, Victoria. I'm sure this is a heart attack.'

'Certainly.'

Mrs Richards' voice was faint but firm. 'I do not — wish to go to hospital, Nurse. I have lived here — happily — since it opened, and I — will die here — happily. Just open the door — so that — I can see the lawns — and the hills and the sky.'

Shelley stared at her, appalled and unsure what to do. 'But I'm not qualified to treat you.'

'I don't want — treatment, girl. You can give me — something — for the pain.' The thin hand was clutching at her chest and throat.

'Where on earth is Miguel, Victoria?' Shelley, appalled at what she was seeing, knew where the morphia was, but hesitated to unlock the cupboard. This was a serious problem, and her instructions were to get any patient in this condition to the city hospital, eight miles away. There were no instructions about what to do if the patient refused to go.

She settled the old lady on a stretcher near the door, so that she could see the sunlit complex, and the happy holidaymakers laughing and shouting as they played in the pool, their conversations a mixture of Spanish and English. She saw Mrs Richards close her eyes in pain, and clutch at the sheet of the stretcher. Shelley didn't wait for Miguel then, but ran to the drug cupboard and unlocked the door. She drew a dose of morphia into a syringe. Professionally cool, maintaining a stolid air of calm in a crisis, she went back to her patient and took her arm. 'This is for the pain, Mrs Richards.'

'Thank you, my — dear.' The old lady lay quiet but tense as the needle delivered its drug. Shelley withdrew it, and covered the site with an antiseptic swab. Slowly the lines of pain smoothed from the old face, and Mrs Richards managed to open her eyes. As the old lady gazed out, over the brilliance of the holiday scene, and beyond, to the rows of white villas, with their deep shadows, and the dark green cypresses dotted between them, up to the ultramarine, cloudless sky, a blissful smile came to her lips. 'Thank you, Nurse. The pain is much better now.'

'Mrs Richards, if you won't let me call an ambulance, I'll have to take you through to the sick bay here, and nurse you myself. It's against my better judgement, you understand?'

'I would like that—but please put me by a window.' The old lady's eyelids were drooping now. The attack was over, but how on earth could Shelley know what damage had been done to the heart muscle? She took the pulse again, listened to the heartbeat, and took the blood-pressure. It was settling. If only Miguel were here, to reassure her that she was doing the right thing.

She looked back at the cupboard, wondering if she ought to give any other heart drugs. Yet there were no symptoms to treat—the old lady was apparently perfectly at peace, her breathing regular and her eyes now closed. Shelley shrugged, and said to Victoria, 'Help me get her into the sick bay. You didn't find Miguel?'

'No, he does not answer his mobile phone.'

'Then I've really no choice. Come on, let's make her as comfortable as possible.' They pushed the trolley through, and positioned it, as the patient had requested, by an open window. There was no electronic monitor, so Shelley would just have to check pulse and blood-pressure regularly. The afternoon was hot and still, the sun's heat lying over the Monte Samana complex like a physical blanket, making even the liveliest of children sleepy. Shelley sat at the patient's bedside while she slept. 'Victoria, do you think you could drive over to Miguel's house and see if he's there?'

'Yes, of course. But do you need him? The Señora Richards looks fine—so peaceful.'

Shelley was slightly exasperated. 'It's one thing being peaceful—it's another thing altogether not knowing if I've done the right thing. Suppose something happens?'

Victoria said softly, 'She is very old, Shelley. She came here to spend her last years happily. Who are we to worry if that is what happens?'

'But I could be accused of negligence! Of giving incorrect treatment! Victoria, I'm worried. Different doctors have different ideas about cardiac treatment.'

'You didn't look worried—you were so calm and kind to her. I was very impressed.'

Shelley shook her head, and began pacing the room. 'I need a second opinion. Where *is* that doctor? He was all over us last week, and now that he's really needed, he's nowhere to be found. Go and get him, Victoria. He's probably at Samana village drinking Sangria with the Freitas family. Leaving me to cope with a situation that is way beyond me!'

Left alone with the patient, Shelley sat down beside the bed, and gradually her head began to nod, and she slid into a sleep oppressed by the heat and by anxiety. When she woke the little room was still quiet, but the sun had moved from the window and was beginning to dip behind the hillside, the cypresses casting long shadows over the tailored lawns. The smell of lighting barbecues drifted in, and the buzz of gentle conversation as guests returned to their villas and apartments to put the children to bed and get changed for the evening.

Her chief's voice merged into her consciousness— smooth and totally without stress. 'Yes, Shelley, you can go off duty now.'

'The hell I can!' Shelley wasn't usually violent, but she had been tested beyond what she thought was right. She jerked into life. 'I'm not leaving this little lady! She came to me, asking me to make sure her life was pleasant! She meant her death, didn't she? Why didn't you leave instructions for me? You must have known——' Thank goodness the patient was asleep.

'Nurse Cameron, do you know who you are speaking to?'

His angry words brought her back to reality, but did nothing to take away her sense of grievance. 'All right,' she spat, afraid of nothing now, resigned to being dismissed, 'I'm speaking to the doctor! To me, the word doctor means total reassurance and trust! How can you look that poor woman in the eye, leaving her to my imperfect care? I did my best, Miguel, but how can my best be worth anything, when the qualified doctor isn't anywhere to be found, and the patient refuses to be moved?'

Miguel Rafaelo didn't react to her tirade. His voice was expressionless. 'Shelley, go and lie down.'

'I told you—I can't, until I know that Mrs Richards is in safe hands.'

'She is in my hands. Now go.'

'I don't consider you a reliable practitioner!'

'I'm all she has, Shelley. Please?'

Shelley saw Victoria Sanchez looking wide-eyed. She realised she was taking Miguel's attention away from his patient. Shelley grabbed her bag, and turned away. 'I'm sorry. I expect my job's gone now. I'll be in my villa if you need me.'

'Shelley——' Miguel was turning to the patient, and Shelley didn't hear what he meant to say. She was finished, she knew. She had been unable to decide what treatment Mrs Richards needed. And on top of that she had been rude to her boss. She walked back to her villa, feeling relief that at last the patient was in reliable hands, and great sadness because she had panicked. Dr Rafaelo would want no more to do with her now. And perhaps it was best. He had made the job here so much more fraught than necessary. First he had disturbed her senses in that first sweet embrace—and now he was making life difficult by not being there when needed, and appearing so much too late. She had never been engaged as an emergency medic, but only as a first-aid post. She felt her heart thump in reaction to the stress she had been under.

Only slowly did her heart-rate come down, and she was able to see that no lasting harm had been done.

Shelley stayed in her villa, regretting the incident, yet blaming her chief for not preparing her for such a patient. It wasn't her fault — yet she had been made to feel guilty. She heard Rosie come, shower, change and go. But she said nothing, as she lay on her bed, her cheeks streaked with dried salt tears; and Rosie went off again, humming a catchy Spanish tune, and smelling of Oscar de la Renta perfume. It was Saturday night, and this was the first time Shelley would miss seeing Miguelito and his flamenco performance at Pepe's Bar.

She found she was straining her ears for the musical clang of the town church bells. The wind was in the right direction, and she heard it strike ten — and then eleven. It would be a pity to miss the handsome young singer. But he had plenty of admirers — and, after all, Shelley Cameron was only one fan. The great Mystery Miguel would scarcely notice if one hysterical female were missing.

Somehow, the spell of the calm evening drew her to her feet. Shelley changed into a fresh dress and stood at the door of the villa. The sound of the start of the midnight bell was clear now through the starlit air, and she was angry with herself for allowing Miguel Rafaelo to prevent her seeing her hero. She was probably going to be fired tomorrow. It would be a shame if she didn't take one last look at her fictional hero — the man it was safe to love because he was so completely out of her world. . .

She closed the door gently behind her and turned towards the road. A quiet voice made her jump. 'Can I give you a lift?' Miguel Rafaelo was waiting, his jeep facing downhill, his face shadowy in the moonlight beneath those graceful cypresses. 'I don't want you to miss the evening's performance.'

She was angry with herself for being ready, for letting him be a witness to her fixation on the handsome young singer. But now that he was here, there was no point in pretending. Her voice was cold. 'Please, if you don't mind. I'd like to catch his act.'

'I'll do my best. Hold on.' And she had never seen the jeep travel so quickly. There was something in the speed, as they rounded corners on two wheels, that shook her out of her bad mood, and when they drew up with a squeal of brakes in the narrow road just by Pepe's Bar, she was laughing at Miguel's uncharacteristic recklessness. But as she shook her hair free and turned to the door, she realised that Miguel was already missing. That was quick. But it was good. She preferred to go in alone.

The church clock was still chiming — ten — eleven — twelve. . . Forgetting Rafaelo, Shelley walked into the bar and elbowed her way towards the dance-floor. She didn't recognise anyone in the shadows, although she knew that she must know several people from Monte Samana. She just wanted to hear her hero's lovely voice, see those flashing eyes and bolster up her imagination with a few of his telling phrases about '*El Amor*'.

And then he was there, singing, his dark hair falling over his face as he plucked passionately at the strings of the guitar. Shelley crept in further, so that she could see his face. It was so well known now, yet it still thrilled her as she saw the way the dim light picked out the shadows of his cheekbones, the sharp angle of his jaw.

She knew that very soon he would break into a flamenco, that the local girls in their frills and flounces would mask him with their castanets and their swinging hips. This was the most precious moment, as he came to the end of his thrilling song, and his gentle but vibrant voice faded away on a note of infinitely passionate promise. . . Shelley stood, rejoicing that she hadn't missed this moment for another week. It might even be the last time she stood there. But reality could wait. Miguel Rafaelo could fire her tomorrow. Today she was here, lost in the beauty of the music of love, and Dr Rafaelo might well not have existed.

The girls didn't flounce on, as the song throbbed away on the night, and the handsome young Miguelito stood upright, wandering into the crowd with a casual roll of the hips, as he strummed his guitar, coaxing yet more sensuous chords from it. He stroked the strings, and before the echo of them died, he said, '*Señorita me quieres?*' Do you love me? There was a loud scream of affirmation, and it was only then, as the audience threatened to swamp him, that the dancing girls came to Miguelito's rescue.

Shelley slipped away then. A fantasy, but a lovely one, and one that she would miss when she went back home. Out in the street, it was almost deserted. Motor-scooters leaned drunkenly against lamp-posts, and idle dogs scavenged, as the sound of flamenco pulsed out from Pepe's Bar. Shelley looked up at the orange moon, slung low behind the ornate roofs of the seaside town. Miguel Rafaelo's jeep was parked under a lamp, and Shelley walked past it. She didn't want to be obliged to him for another lift. She set off for Monte Samana alone.

Her thoughts now were happy ones — warm, imaginary ones. '*Me quieres?*' Do you love me? Surely he didn't need to ask. The audience of willing females had shouted the answer so loudly that it could probably have been heard back in Monte Samana.

And then the screech of brakes. 'Get in, Shelley! Someone wants help.'

She got into the jeep without question. Miguel Rafaelo thrust on the accelerator. 'There is a nurse supervising Mrs Richards,' he said. 'She called just now to say someone has collapsed outside the medical centre.'

Shelley said, 'You don't think it's drink again? The last time I was called from here it was a false alarm.'

'Impossible to say.' His voice was almost drowned in the roar of third gear, as they turned into the floodlit gateway of the Monte Samana complex. 'Hold tight, Shelley!' And as they roared along the tailored pathways, she found herself hearing not 'Impossible to say' but '*Me quieres?*'

'*Me quieres?*' Do you love me? Shelley held on tight to the seatbelt, and looked sideways at Miguel. The light glinted on his glasses as yet again they rounded corners on two wheels. Within seconds he had screeched to a halt at the medical centre, and her fanciful ideas had vanished in the haste of their rush to help.

It was a genuine emergency—the nurse from the village had put the patient on a couch in the examining-room, and she quickly explained in Spanish what had happened. 'She fell down some steps, Doctor. I do not think the ankle is broken, but very badly sprained. Maybe she requires an X-ray?'

Shelley had already gone to the patient and was holding the swollen ankle. As Miguel came towards her, Shelley said, 'A good firm bandage, I think. And no weight-bearing. We can get the test done tomorrow.'

'You're right, Shelley—except that we don't request X-rays on Sundays unless the condition is life-threatening. It will have to wait until Monday.'

'Well, she can't walk.'

'Right. But as Consuelo is already kindly supervising here, we can give her another patient for the night.'

Shelley said, 'There's no need. I've had a rest, I'll take over from her.'

'I won't hear of it. Consuelo would be angry if you took away her chance to earn a little fee.'

'Are you sure?'

'Would I lie to you?'

Again she didn't hear the words he said, but an echo of the handsome singer—'*Me quieres?*' Do you love me? And Shelley shook her head to clear it. Was she so very tired that she couldn't distinguish one man's voice from another's? 'I really don't know.'

'Come, Shelley, I'll drive you home.'

'No, thank you.'

'I won't touch you!' His voice lilted as he teased her a little. 'I'm tired too, you know.'

'I'd rather walk. It's probably my last time.'

'Last time?'

'You're going to fire me, aren't you? After I shouted at you for not being there for Mrs Richards?'

Miguel said quietly, 'We Spaniards are always shouting, Shelley—it is our way of life. If you are angry, then you shout. It is natural, and it is quickly forgotten. And we do not bottle up the emotions.' He reached out a hand, conciliatorily. 'Let us walk up and discuss philosophy in the moonlight.'

And then she noticed his sleeve under the hastily pulled-on sweater, and her step faltered. His shirt was red silk, and the sleeves were full and flamboyant. It was a shirt exactly like the one her singer had been wearing that night, as he swaggered among the women, and whispered '*Me quieres?*' to them all.

Miguel asked, 'What's the matter? Why did you stop walking?'

'It's—nothing.' Many Spanish men wore gaudy clothes. It was traditional, and it suited them. But Miguel Rafaelo? He had always seemed so stuffy and plain in his dress. 'Nothing at all.' Why shouldn't he wear a red shirt on his day off? But the colour—so exact. And the fine quality silk, catching the moonlight just as Miguelito's sleeve had done. . . Shelley pulled herself together. The two men were so different that it must be just a coincidence. She said, 'It's a hot night. Why are you wearing a sweater?'

'Because it looks more proper when I am looking after a patient.'

'I see.' That made sense. She asked him another question, as he didn't seem to mind. 'Did I really give Mrs Richards the right treatment?'

'Yes, exactly right.'

'But you shouldn't have left me alone.'

'I've seen you at work, Shelley. I knew you could be trusted.'

'You should have told me about Mrs Richards' heart condition—and about her request not to be moved from Monte Samana. I didn't know if it was right or not.'

Miguel said gravely, 'Was not Victoria there?'

'Yes, she was.'

'Victoria knew. There was no need for me to be there too. I was aware that I could trust you in a crisis. That's what I pay you for.'

'I suppose that's a compliment.'

He nodded, and for the first time paused and looked into her eyes. 'It is a compliment.'

'Then thank you.'

He smiled, and she thought how even and white his smile was. 'Well done, Shelley. You have accepted a compliment gracefully, without trying to pretend you don't deserve it. We are making progress after all!'

'Oh, I deserve it, all right! Anyone who can work with you deserves a medal, never mind a compliment!'

He laughed, and as they began their walk he put his arm very lightly round her shoulders. It was such a non-threatening touch that she allowed him to leave it there.

She said, 'You know, you keep very brief records on your patients. If Mrs Richards has been here so long, she ought to have some kind of permanent record, to help new staff like me.'

'This is a holiday place, and some people only come

once. Most people are never ill. I'm not running a hospital, Shelley, only a first-aid post.'

'Well, I've kept detailed records.'

'I know, and it is good—but we will probably never use them again, so next season they will be forgotten.'

'That's very casual. What if a mistake is made?'

'Victoria is always there.'

'You seem to place a lot of trust in Victoria.'

'I do. She is invaluable.' Miguel's voice was suddenly very warm, and Shelley remembered that he and his beautiful young assistant had been close for some time.

They reached the plateau where Rosie's villa stood in a row of similar ones. As on that first night, Shelley looked down at the glowing rectangle of blue that was the floodlit pool. The barbecue had gone out by now, and the singer had long packed up her keyboard. Shelley said, 'I'm glad I'm not being fired. And I'm sorry I shouted at you.'

'Don't mention it. I am glad. As I told you, it means you are becoming more Spanish! What is that word that describes you British so well? Uptight, that's what you are! Well, you are beginning to lose it, and as a medical man I assure you it will do you more good than harm.'

His voice was calm and friendly, and Shelley was feeling happy because she had seen Miguelito again, and he had looked into her eyes when he asked '*Me quieres?*' She said, 'Thanks for walking me home, and thank you again for taking me to Pepe's.'

'It was a pleasure. We will go again some time—maybe we will speak with your hero afterwards, *no*?'

'Really? Do you really mean it?'

'Oh, yes, Shelley. I may not be very reliable in your eyes——'

She protested, 'I didn't mean it, honestly——'

'Well, perhaps not. But I will keep my word, my dear—I can see just how much it means to you.'

'I'd like that.'

He paused and said, his glasses catching the glint of the moon, 'Naturally, if you come to your senses and stop hero-worshipping him, then there will be no need to introduce you to the empty-headed young pup.'

She knew he was teasing her, so she didn't react sharply, merely said, 'Oh yes there will. Even when I stop idolising him, I'd still like to be able to tell him what pleasure his lovely voice has given me all these Saturday evenings.'

'I suppose he does know how to handle a guitar,' said Miguel casually. 'I'll allow him that. Did you notice that he actually came out and spoke to his audience tonight?'

'Yes — that was unexpected — but he got the reaction he wanted, I think — the screams of adoration from his fans.'

'Did you reply to his question, Shelley? Did you reply, "Yes, I love you, Miguelito"?'

'No.'

'Oh, dear, then you are still too uptight.'

'I'm not quite as silly as you think I am, Miguel.'

He faced her in the moonlight, and he was smiling. 'I never said I thought that. I know you are a sensible woman — most of the time.'

She smiled back. It was too late to argue. 'Thank you again for bringing me home.' She turned and walked slowly up to the front door of the villa. There she stopped and turned. Miguel stood where she had left him, outlined against the star-studded sky, and there was something about the way he was standing that reminded her of someone else. . .

She was still awake when she heard Rosie coming in. 'Hi, had a good evening?'

'You didn't tell me that Francisco had hurt himself.'

'I'm sorry, Rosie. I was lying down when you came in this evening. It's been a long day. Is Francisco all right?'

'Yes, he's fine. He said you were very kind to him,

you and Miguel—hardly hurt him at all.' Rosie sat on the bed. 'You came to Pepe's with Miguel, didn't you?'

'He gave me a lift, that's all. It wasn't a date or anything—he just came to take me there. And we had to come back together because a guest had twisted her ankle and it needed bandaging.'

'I see.'

'I'm not chasing him, and I'm not going to be number four, Rosie. You'll see—I'll probably not see him for the rest of the week.'

'OK, I'll believe you. But I'd hate it if you got hurt.'

'I'm becoming more Spanish, Rosie—not so uptight about everything.'

Her friend laughed. 'Do you know, I believe you are!'

'And Miguel is going to introduce me to Miguelito!'

'Never! Lucky old Shelley—the first woman to meet him face to face.' She slipped her shoes off. 'I wonder if he'll finally allow his identity to be revealed? Your Dr Rafaelo must be a very important man if he can promise you that.'

Shelley looked at her friend. 'But Rosie, you've worked here for years. You mean you don't know that Miguel——'

'That Miguel what?'

'Nothing. Who owns Monte Samana, Rosie? Who does your father rent your shop from?'

'It's a consortium. There's an agent in Cartagena who handles all the letting and selling.'

'I see.' Miguel had really entrusted her with a great secret. Shelley was beginning to see that she had been put in a very special place of importance in Miguel's confidence. 'Has Miguel Rafaelo always been the doctor here?'

'Oh, yes.'

'And has Mystery Miguelito been at Pepe's for long?'

'What are you getting at, Shelley? He's been at Pepe's as long as I've been coming here — though he does sometimes take holidays, I must admit.'

Shelley was sitting up in bed, her arms round her knees. She said, 'I wonder why Miguel Rafaelo isn't married.'

'He's good-looking, I agree, but you said it yourself, Shelley — he's wrapped up in his work. He's not a fun-loving person.'

'No, he's not got much time for anything but work. And yet — and yet — tonight we. . .'

'No, Shelley, no! You are not to fall for him, and that's an order!'

'There's no danger of that, I assure you, Rosie, dear.' Shelley was superior in her rejection of Rosie's fantasies. 'We're just good friends——'

'Isn't that the classic white lie?'

'Not in my case, I swear it. I've seen just how important Victoria Sanchez is to him, Rosie. When Miguel Rafaelo decides it's time to settle down, Victoria will be the girl, I'm certain of it, Rosie.'

'Yes, I think I agree with you. She is always there, isn't she? And never with another man. Victoria it will be.'

And Shelley lay back that night, watching the fan sway round and round above her, and wishing that Rosie's certainty hadn't been quite so fervent. A little hesitation would have been in order.

She had almost given Miguel's secret away. Soon she would be the proud keeper of two secrets — the first that Miguel Rafaelo owned Monte Samana, and second that she, Shelley Cameron, would be the only woman to know the true identity of the famous Miguelito. Shelley hugged herself in the moonlight, and felt very privileged.

CHAPTER FIVE

SHELLEY heard the church bells in the distance next morning, and woke feeling the beauty of the peaceful Spanish hillsides, the gentle village in the valley, with its easygoing, friendly inhabitants. Slowly, very slowly, she was becoming part of it. Even more part of it than Rosie, who had been coming for years. It was a very satisfactory feeling, and she threw back the sheet to feel the caressing warmth of the morning on her body.

Rosie was still sleeping. Shelley cut a grapefruit in half and squeezed the juice. Then she took the glass of juice, a cup of black coffee and a slice of crusty toast and butter, and sat outside on the balcony. The sun was just catching the summit of the opposite hillside, making a corona of light over the towering cypresses. Sparrows twittered and quarrelled, and paused to pick up crumbs right by Shelley's feet.

'This is the life.' It was hard to remember being cold, rushed, flurried and upset. If she wished, Shelley could remain here, working with the people of Santa Barbara and of Samana, and never go back to all the heartache and the pain of her old job. True, she was important back home, while here she was just a small cog in the wheel of Samana life. But wasn't it better this way? She thought of Miguel, stern, slightly stuffy at times, yet so kind and so intelligent. And she thought of him relaxed, as he had been on the beach, his incredible body beside hers as they ran down to the sea, his face laughing and his hair untidy. . . Could she work alongside Miguel, and stay as she was today, aloof and immune to his attractions as a man?

My favourite wardrobe. She smiled, as she drained her coffee and threw the rest of the crumbs to the sparrows. How could she have called him that? The telephone trilled politely, and she ran to get it before it disturbed Rosie. '*Sí. Buenos días.*'

'Shelley, this is Consuelo. Can you come down, please?'

'Is there a patient?'

'No, no patient. But there are some drugs missing from the cupboard, and I thought I see you before I telephone to Dr Rafaelo.'

Shelley's good mood vanished with the morning mist. The drug cupboard! She had been the last to use it, when she unlocked it to get the morphia for Mrs Richards. 'I'll be there in a jiffy.'

Consuelo greeted her calmly as she arrived, breathless from running down the hill. 'I give breakfast to the patients.'

'I'd better see them first. How is Mrs Richards?'

'Well. And the other *señora*, she also feel much better. The ankle is not now so swollen.'

'Then it can't be broken. That's good.' Shelley went in to speak quietly to her patients, trying to push to the back of her mind the knowledge that she might have left the drug cupboard open in her anxiety yesterday.

'Nurse Shelley, I want to thank you for caring for me,' said the old lady.

'Mrs Richards, it's my job. But I wish I'd known you'd given orders that you didn't want to be moved to hospital.'

The old lady smiled, her face no longer strained, but lively and tanned, the eyes bright. 'To tell you the truth, I wouldn't mind if yesterday had been my last day. When I awoke this morning, I felt a teeny twinge of regret that I was still here.'

Shelley understood. In spite of the worry at the back of her mind, she sat down beside her patient and said gently, 'As I sat having my breakfast to the sound of church bells, with the sun coming up behind the hills,

I think I felt the sort of affinity you must have with Samana. It's to be surrounded by beauty, isn't it? I'm sure life and death both seem pleasant in such a place.'

'You put it very well, my dear. Well, since God has decreed that I don't die just yet, I look forward to getting to know you better.'

'That's something I look forward to as well.' Shelley smiled down. 'Is there anything I can get you?'

'Nothing. Go and speak with Consuelo — she's looking very jumpy about something.'

'I will. See you later, Mrs Richards.' Shelley left the two women in the sunny little sickroom and went through to where Consuelo sat at the desk. 'What's missing, Consuelo?'

'The morphia. And some analgesic tablets. I think that is all.'

'Analgesics?'

'The ones that were mentioned in a TV programme last week. A girl in the soap opera committed suicide with them. I always think it is not wise to name drugs on television.'

'Perhaps. But it's common knowledge, I suppose. I wish I knew what time they were taken. I know I unlocked the cupboard to get the morphia at about eleven in the morning.'

'Did you lock it straight afterwards?'

'I think so, because I checked the door later before going down to the village, and it was locked then, and the key was in my purse.'

'Then the drugs must have been taken then, unless it was during this morning when I unlocked the cupboard with Dr Rafaelo's key to take out anti-inflammatory tablets for Señora Thorpe.'

'That was when you realised that there were two empty spaces in the cupboard?'

'Yes.' Consuelo looked anxious. 'I think we must report this to the police.'

'You're right, of course. I'll telephone Dr Rafaelo.

Let's just hope that whoever took those drugs hasn't done anything with them.' Shelley went to the phone, wishing she didn't have to wake Miguel with such bad news. She tapped out his number, wondering which room of that little hillside hacienda was the one where he slept.

'Yes, Shelley?' His voice sounded pleasantly rested, warm and pleased to hear her.

'I'm sorry, Miguel, but some morphia and some analgesics are missing from the drug cupboard. Shall I call the police?'

His voice changed. 'Wait until I get there.'

'Yes, Doctor.'

'I am on my way.'

'I'm very sorry.'

'It may not be anyone's fault.' He rang off, and it was only minutes before they heard the chug of the engine of his jeep coming down from the hills in the still of the morning.

Miguel must have rung the *policía*, because their car drew up at the same time as Miguel's jeep. The young constable was polite and thorough, as he arranged for the cupboard door to be dusted for fingerprints. 'Is there anyone in Monte Samana whom you know to be a suspect, Dr Rafaelo?'

Miguel shook his head. 'Most of the staff are regulars. I do not suspect them—although naturally you must do your job and make sure they are questioned. I think it must be an opportunist thief, someone just passing by—nobody knew the cupboard was going to be open just at that time.'

Shelley said miserably, 'I feel responsible for this. Didn't you say that those youths who got their friend drunk the other Saturday were not the kind of visitors you liked here?'

'I did. Well remembered, Shelley.' Miguel turned to Victoria, who had appeared while the policeman was checking the surgery, and said, 'Please find out which apartments those youths are in. If they live near to Mrs Richards's villa, then one of them might have slipped down in the confusion to see what he could find in the surgery.'

Victoria went to look for the schedules of the complex from the main office. Shelley said, 'Shall I ask Mrs Richards if she noticed anyone?'

'If she is well enough.'

'I'll ask her gently.' Shelley went through. Mrs Richards was dozing, but she opened her eyes when Shelley went near. 'When you were taken ill, Mrs Richards, were you alone?'

'I was in the café by the pool.'

'It was mid-morning. Was the pool being used?'

'Yes, there were some lads in there, fooling around.'

Shelley nodded, satisfied that her hunch could be correct. 'Thank you. Rest now.' She went back to Miguel and reported the news. 'There were some boys nearby when she was first taken ill.'

Miguel looked at the policeman, who made a note in his book. 'I will interview them first. Do not warn them — I will just go to their apartment. It is early, so they are probably still sleeping.' He paused and added, 'If anyone took them, they must have been clever — there are no fingerprints to be found, apart from the two nurses'.' Miguel and Victoria accompanied him, to show him which apartment he needed. But first Miguel sent Shelley to Santa Barbara village. 'I'm worried about Abuelo, Shelley,' he told her. 'He was sitting in the village street, and I had no time to stop and see to him. He may have been there all night.'

'I'll go at once. Shall I take the jeep?'

'Yes, please.'

It had started as a peaceful day, but had rapidly turned into one of the busiest and most worrying. Shelley took the medical bag and swung herself into the jeep. She was wearing white cotton jeans, a peach-coloured T-shirt and white tennis shoes. The residents of Monte Samana were just beginning to stir, and the smell of strong Spanish coffee wafted from open windows and balconies as she drove along the flower-edged lanes of the complex and out of the main gate towards the village.

The road led between lemon groves, and beyond them the sea sparkled in the distance. But Shelley was concentrating on the mystery of the drug cupboard, and wondering what old Abuelo Freitas was doing sitting in the village street all night.

He was there, his head in its black beret nodding over his chest, sitting at one of the outdoor tables of the village café under spreading broad-leaved plane trees. There was an empty earthenware wine jug on the table, and two used glasses. His battered black pipe lay by the glass. Shelley sat next to him, and touched his hand.

'He is all right, Señorita Shelley.' María, the young woman who kept the bar, was just coming back from church, her head still covered by a black lace mantilla. 'He met his cousin last night, and they drank too much wine, but do not worry—it is not the first time he spends the night like this.' She smiled at his sleeping form. 'He and his cousin, they reminisce about the war. Abuelo had a tough time, they say.'

'But what do his daughter and granddaughter say?'

'They leave him. He comes to no harm.' The woman smiled and said, 'Will you have some coffee? I will bring two, in case he wakes up.'

Shelley was reassured, but she still felt that Abuelo Freitas was sitting too still. She felt his pulse. It was regular, but was it fainter than usual? When Maria brought out two cups of coffee, Shelley said, 'You know, I think he has emphysema. Chest trouble brought on by years of holding that smelly old pipe in his mouth while he talks.'

'I know this. But he is an old man, *señorita*. He cannot change his habits now.'

'You're telling me not to interfere, aren't you?'

'It is kind of you to care.'

'I'm only following Dr Rafaelo's orders.'

Maria sat beside them at the table. 'Would you like me to fetch Dolores, his daughter?'

'Well, yes — I can't leave him unless I know he's all right.'

Maria shook her head. 'You all take things too seriously, *señorita*. Even Dr Rafaelo is not yet completely a southerner. He is from Madrid, and although he has lived among us for many years now, he still thinks like a *madrileño* sometimes.'

'It's the way he thinks — the way he cares.'

'I know that, Señorita Shelley, and we are grateful for what he does here. You too — you spend time amongst us as if you were our sister.'

Shelley admitted it. 'I love being here.' She leaned over and touched old Freitas again. 'Abuelito — Grandfather — wake up and tell us you are all right.'

There was a rattling sound as old Freitas started to cough. Shelley shook her head in mock despair at the state of his lungs, but she was reassured by the noise, and the way he sat up straight and opened his eyes, blinking in the brightness of the morning sun beneath the plane tree shade. Abuelo said, coughing, 'It is Shelley, is it, waking me at this unearthly hour?'

Maria said sharply, 'Unearthly! You have missed morning church, Abuelito. You should be ashamed of yourself! You see how Dr Rafaelo sent Señorita Shelley to make sure you were all right!'

He reached for his pipe. 'Send Dolores to get me some tobacco.'

But it was his granddaughter, fresh-faced Lina, four months pregnant, who came to bring her grandfather. 'Mother says he cannot smoke in the house while I am with child.'

'That's wise,' said Shelley. 'The smoke can harm the little one.'

Abuelo Freitas coughed and said, 'Now you see why I have to sleep in the street!'

'Abuelito, you do not! All you must do is leave your pipe unlit in the house.'

The old man drank his coffee and muttered, 'I have lived through many cruel things, child, and now you are cruel to your *abuelito*.'

Shelley had been watching them, amused at this family banter, knowing that it was no business of hers to stay, now that she knew the old man was all right. 'I think I can leave you to your granddaughter's care, Abuelito. I'm glad you've come to no harm, spending the night in the street.'

'It is not the first time, and it won't be the last,' he laughed. And he reached out and took her hand. 'Thank you. Thank you for caring about a useless old man.'

As they had been chatting, other villagers had drifted out into the warmth of the sun. Children came out to play see-saw with an old plank they had found at the roadside. Two goats grazed between the tables, and looked with mild brown eyes to see if there was anything worth stealing from the tables. Shelley was reluctant to go back. She finished her coffee, and gazed up at the hillside, where Rafaelo's white villa caught the sun, and his growing vegetables and vines lay in neat terraces up the hill. The thought of living here in this gentle setting appealed to her. These villagers lived alongside the modern world, the developed complex of Monte Samana, and the growing beach hotels and windsurfing bases that were sprouting by the week along the seafront. Yet they didn't change their lives, and no one tried to make them. They were happy. It was clear why Miguel had chosen Santa Barbara as the site for his development.

The handsome young fisherman Pablo had joined them in the café, and now he said, '*Señorita*, you are doing nothing today. Let me take you out in my boat, and show you where I catch my *mero*.'

'That would be nice, but I must report back to Dr Rafaelo.'

'Why? You work today also?'

'I work while the hospital is open. Consuelo can't carry on all day, when she's stayed there all night. I must get back.'

'I think the doctor make you work too hard!'

'No, I enjoy my work.'

'*Señorita, señorita*!' A cry from further down the street, and a woman Shelley hadn't met before came running. 'My little son — is bitten by a dog. Please come, *señorita*.'

Shelley ran to the jeep for the medical bag. 'All right, I'm coming. Is it your own dog, or a stray?' The thought of rabies wasn't far away.

'It belongs to the farmer. Pedro pulled its tail.'

Then it was probably safe, but Shelley was taking no chances. She went into the shadowy house, where a boy of about four was holding his arm. Teeth marks showed clearly where the dog had bitten, but it had hardly broken the skin. Shelley cleaned the wound very thoroughly and bound it up with a clean dressing. Then she took a syringe out and gave the boy an anti-tetanus jab. 'You will need two more of these,' she told him.

'You will do it for me?' His big black eyes were trusting now. 'You do not hurt me.'

'Yes, I'll come and do it for you. And don't pull dogs' tails any more, will you?'

A man's voice from the doorway made her turn. 'I'm sure he won't.' Miguel stood there, and she was absurdly glad to see him. He said, 'If you have finished, I'd like some lunch.'

Outside in the afternoon heat reflected in the dusty road, Shelley said, 'Did you find the drugs?'

'The police are investigating.' He smiled slightly. 'You have had a busy morning?'

'Yes. I was just coming back when the child was bitten.'

'There's no hurry. Consuelo insists that she slept well last night, and is happy to stay on today. Would you like to have lunch with me?'

'Yes, thank you.'

'You have not explored the surrounding countryside, I know, because you have been working so hard. We'll go to one of my favourite restaurants — a typical Spanish Sunday lunch. It starts at three. First we go to my villa for a drink and a siesta.'

'Oh, but —'

'Shelley, Shelley, why are you jumping like a little flea? You wish for a cool drink on my shady patio, do you not?'

'Yes, I do.'

'Then say so! Come!' And he led the way to the jeep, waving to the people in the café, and pausing to chat to Maria as she served a tray full of beer, and to Abuelo as his granddaughter led him away by the hand.

Shelley did not confess that she had driven past the Casa Madrid. It was simple but very elegant through that carved stone gateway, the courtyard roofed in by vines twining over wires, so that the chairs and tables were shielded from the sun's extreme heat by the delicate leaves. A quiet woman in a large white apron brought them cold white wine in a red earthenware jug, and they sat at the edge of the patio looking out at the rows of vines, of lemon trees, tomatoes and capsicums that straggled down the hillside, shaded in places by tall cypresses and stunted white-trunked olive trees.

'Well, do you like it?' he asked.

'How could anyone not like it? It's perfect.'

'It's intended to be. But I find it can be lonely.'

Shelley smiled, and sipped at the cool wine. 'Then you must get married, Miguel, and fill this lovely courtyard with *niños*.'

'You recommend that, do you?'

'If you're lonely, that is the answer.'

'It's very final, marriage.'

'It's meant to be. If you feel afraid, then you're not ready.'

He smiled at her, the light in the black eyes hidden by his sunglasses. 'You sound like an expert.'

'It doesn't take much expertise to know that.'

'You aren't ready, are you, Shelley?'

'No.'

'Want to tell me?' His voice was very gentle.

She knew she would have to tell him one day, and now seemed a good time. 'There's not much to tell. I dated a man—a doctor. His name was Ken, and he wasn't the right man for me. He was very concerned about his sexual prowess—and I found his attitude towards women crude and very thoughtless.'

'Something like that puts you off men?'

'I think that's perfectly natural, don't you?'

'Yes. Yes, I do, Shelley.'

She went on, somehow bewitched by the enchantment of the surroundings into feeling totally relaxed. 'I thought my life was over, and that I'd never be able to have a relationship again. That was very foolish, because relationships aren't everything. I've never been as peaceful and happy as I am here.'

'Without any relationships?'

'Yes. It's good for the soul.'

'What would you do if Miguelito fell for you?'

'He wouldn't.'

'Why not? He has to settle down and marry one day, just as I do, hasn't he?'

'Yes, Miguel, I dare say he has. But not with a cold-hearted spinster from Northumberland. He'll fall for a luscious, hot-blooded Spanish girl who understands his music and can match him in passion.'

'You could be right.' Miguel had been watching her, and she realised that she had been talking far too freely, and that she couldn't see what he was thinking because of those dark glasses. He stood up suddenly. 'Come — I'm hungry.'

She rose to her feet, and looked down again at the rolling hillside covered with fruit and vegetables, with grazing goats, sheep and chickens. Miguel stood beside her, watching her. She said, 'It's so perfect. I think maybe I must have been Spanish in some former life — I feel as though I've come home.'

His voice was low and vibrant. 'And you said you were a cold-hearted spinster? Shelley, Shelley, you may know medicine, but you certainly don't know yourself.'

She laughed, and turned to him. 'Maybe not, Miguel, but you're doing your best to teach me, aren't you? You want to psycho-analyse me and send me home with all my little idiosyncrasies ironed out!' He took off his glasses and put his arms around her waist, and they stood for a while facing one another. Shelley didn't feel threatened by him now. They had laughed and talked as friends, and that was how she saw him. She said calmly, 'And kissing me isn't going to iron anything out. You'd do better to go and find someone beautiful and lively to marry who can cook and keep house and look after this little paradise of yours.'

'Are you saying you are a lost cause? Just because your first relationship didn't work?'

'I'm not right for you, and we both know it.'

'We'll see about that.' His grip tightened about her, and he caught her head in his hand, turning her face to his. Then he seemed to think of something, and said, 'Why did you say I needed someone lively? Am I boring, Shelley?'

She burst out laughing. 'No, no, you aren't boring, Miguel.'

'A wardrobe, maybe?'

She shook her head, exasperated with him. 'Not a wardrobe. You're nice, really you are.'

'Kiss me, then.'

She looked deep into the black eyes. 'Just as a friend?'

'Of course just as a friend! You think I want to elope with you?'

She raised her face to his then, and reached out to catch his lips with her own. It was meant to be swift and brief, but the moment she touched him Miguel took control, and kissed her long and hard, so that she found herself breathing deeply, gasping for air. Had she really been so innocent that she'd forgotten how passionately he could kiss?

And at once all the warnings flooded back into her mind. Number four nurse. The fourth to be hurt, while Victoria Sanchez waited patiently on the sidelines, knowing that one day Miguel would realise how much he loved her and wanted her to be mistress of the Casa Madrid. Shelley drew back from Miguel's hungry mouth. 'That's enough psycho-analysis for one day.' She tried to keep her voice steady, though her feelings were doing somersaults inside her.

His arms were still round her, and his smile lit up his face. Somehow she had disturbed his hair, and it fell boyishly over his forehead. For a moment she felt a violent pain in her heart—as though she was falling in love. . . Then he said innocently, 'You started it!' And he let her go quickly, so that she stumbled, and he had to reach out to steady her.

She said breathlessly, 'Shall we go?'

'We'd better.' He was still holding her arm, and she was very aware that it would be the easiest thing in the world to embrace him again, while he was still looking so handsome. He smiled again. 'It's either lunch, or an afternoon of —'

'Lunch,' she said hastily. 'What about this restaurant that you couldn't wait to show me?'

'Let's go.' Miguel smoothed back his hair over his ears, put on the dark glasses, and reached for the keys to the jeep.

It was a large wooden building, with no ceiling but cool crisscrossed rafters going up into the roof of wood and thatch. It was full of long tables that seated from six and eight to a dozen or more. Most tables were full of large extended Spanish families, with tots in high chairs, to the most aged of black-clad grannies. Waiters ran around from table to table, shouting to each other and to the customers, so fast that Shelley couldn't catch what was going on. 'Don't worry, I'll order for us,' said Miguel. They had found a small table tucked in between three long ones, and had already been given a jug of iced water, a long loaf, a pot of butter and a plate of olives. Miguel sampled an olive. 'Hmm, not bad, but not as good as mine.' He pushed the dish towards Shelley, but she shook her head. Miguel asked, 'What is the matter?'

She couldn't tell him. It had been easy to be friends when she hadn't felt this sudden urgent longing for him. But today had shown her that she wasn't immune to normal natural feelings, and even her imaginery passion for the handsome singer hadn't protected her from this very real and very frightening feeling of genuine affection. She didn't look at him now, but stared at her plate, and nibbled at a piece of fresh bread as a way of avoiding conversation.

'Shelley?'

'Yes?'

'What is the matter?' he asked again.

'Don't — order too much. I don't think I'm terribly hungry.'

'Trust me. You'll be hungry when you see what I order.' But his eyes behind the glasses were kindly and understanding, and she fervently hoped they weren't reading her thoughts.

A central dish of salad was brought first, followed by fresh seafood and grilled *mero* with slices of lemon, tomato and garlic and two tender chunks of swordfish. Shelley didn't touch the wine, but stuck to the iced water, in between delicious mouthfuls of the fish, which she had to admit was absolute perfection, the best she had ever tasted.

Gradually she regained her composure. But it had shattered her to realise just how vulnerable she was, and she kept the conversation very brittle and light, to cover up her own inadequacy. 'Did you know, Miguel, that the people of Santa Barbara think you're uptight? Yes, you, Señor Cool himself!'

'Me? Rubbish, woman. I am a villager myself!'

'Shall I tell you what they think? What they told me this morning?'

'Yes, go ahead. I'll show you if I'm uptight or not!' He pretended to be angry.

She tried to relax, smiling, and toying with her glass. 'When I went to old Abuelo Freitas, Maria told me that you sometimes worried too much about him—that you didn't understand that he only wanted to be left alone. Now if that isn't being uptight, then I don't know what is.'

'Oh, Shelley, that's nonsense and you know it. I know the old man sometimes falls asleep over his wine. But he is old, Shelley, and he has to come to his end some time. I was only thinking of the family—they would wish to bring the priest in good time.' Shelley didn't reply to this, and he realised she was smiling at him, teasing him. 'You made me rise to that bait, didn't you?'

'Maybe.' The electricity between them was becoming unbearable, their light-hearted words so obviously hiding something deeper. For a long moment they both stopped eating, and looked across the table at each other. Shelley was conscious of the sound of her own breathing, even amid the clatter of plates and the loud hubbub of Spanish conversation. She said in a low voice, 'Please take me home. I'm sorry, Miguel, but I want to go back now.'

'I understand.' He came round the table to help her up. He signalled to the waiter that he had put two twenty-peseta notes on the table, and led her out into the afternoon sun. 'It's been a long day. I'm sorry — I was selfish, to try to monopolise you.'

'It wasn't you. I'm just feeling a bit — tired.'

They stopped at the jeep, and he eyed her solemnly. 'Would you like to take the jeep yourself? Keep it at Monte Samana. I can easily get a lift back to my house.'

'Thanks.' She took the keys from him, and was appalled to hear them rattle in her shaking hand. 'I'll be fine,' she added, as he took a step towards her. 'I'll see you tomorrow, then. Thank you for lunch — it really was lovely.'

'Next time you'll enjoy it even more.' Miguel waited while she climbed up into the driver's seat and wrapped on the seat belt. 'I meant what I said, Shelley — I do understand, you know, why you must go.'

Shelley managed a smile. 'I'm just tired.' But she knew that Miguel did understand a lot about her — sometimes possibly more than she did herself. He would recognise that she was running away from him.

CHAPTER SIX

MRS RICHARDS confided in Shelley, 'Because you have such a sweet and caring face, my dear.'

Shelley shook her head. 'I'm a sister, so I'm bound to be a dragon.'

'Maybe it takes one to know one! I've been called a dragon in my time, Shelley, but in my case I've knowingly been an old crosspatch sometimes.'

'I've never seen you cross.'

'That's because I came to live here. Mine is a sad story, Shelley, but I feel you'd understand it.' Mrs Richards was allowed to sit on a chair by the window, her thin body almost recovered from the heart attack. Victoria had been playing gin rummy with her, and Shelley had come to take over. Mrs Richards said, 'You aren't a dragon, and I don't intend to allow you to become one. It isn't fun, being a dragon, believe me.'

'You can stop it happening?'

'I can tell you my story.'

'Yes, tell me. But don't forget to drink your vitamins.'

The old lady picked up the glass and pulled a face. 'Why does everything that's good for you taste ghastly? Anyway, Shelley, I think you ought to take some of this. In spite of your tan, you're looking a bit peaky, my dear.'

'I'm the nurse!' Shelley pretended to be severe, and her patient meekly drank her medicine and handed back the glass.

Mrs Richards stared unseeing out of the window. It was a typical late afternoon scene, with the pool full of children playing ball, splashing and laughing, the older ones talking confidentially while holding on to the side, perhaps making assignations that they would have to negotiate with parents to keep. The old lady said, 'I came back here because over fifty years ago this is where I first fell in love.'

'But Monte Samana didn't exist then.'

'No, Shelley, it didn't. There was just a small village inn — it was over there, where the administration block is now. My parents were fond of travel, and they'd brought me on a trip, long before people had even heard of package holidays. We had a large car — a Humber, with leopardskin seat covers. I was bored between stops, but when we came to Santa Barbara I fell in love with the lovely cove, with the village — and with the local farmer's son.'

'A holiday romance?'

'Much more than that, Shelley.' Mrs Richards paused, and the old eyes were unseeing as she remembered. 'Much, much more than that. He waited for me every year — we came back for about six years, until I was ready to be sent to finishing school. Oh, yes, I was only a girl, and he was only a boy — but when my mother told me we wouldn't be coming back, and that I'd very soon forget him, I believed her.' The old lady's voice tailed off. 'I believed her when she assured me I would meet someone much more suitable when it was time for me to get married.'

'And you didn't?'

'I met Clive Richards. I married Clive because Mummy told me he was suitable for me, and I hadn't had a letter from Felipe for a long time. . . It turned out he was missing in action. Oh, Shelley, Clive was a nice enough person and he was always good to me, but he wasn't right for me, and although I appeared to live happily I used to long for things to be as they were between Felipe and me. And then Felipe came back after the war, and I knew I should have believed in myself and waited for him. Of course,' the old lady's voice faltered, 'one did, in those days, listen to one's parents more.'

'Where's Felipe now?'

Mrs Richards turned and looked at her, and there were tears in the pale blue eyes. 'I believe he's in the village — with his wife and his daughter and his granddaughter. He seems contented — if he is the right man.'

'Have you — spoken to him?'

'No, no. I never go there. Why try to rekindle the past? He has made his life, and it's almost over — like mine. It's too late to remind him of what is long gone.'

'And so you came to live here after you were widowed?'

'Yes. Somehow I find a little peace of mind knowing that I'm in the one place in the world where I once knew true happiness.'

'That's sad. I suppose you're lucky to have been happy, though, even for a short time. Some people never meet the right one even once.'

'That's what I think too. I am lucky in my way. But it still makes me bitter and angry at the waste, the terrible waste of all that love I had. Where did it go, Shelley? I just became a vinegary old dragon, and all my bitterness turned in on myself and affected my heart. Now you see why I'll be quite content to slip away when God calls me to go.'

'I do see.'

'Are you in love, Shelley?'

She started, not expecting a personal question. Then she smiled and replied to the question with a joke. 'Not exactly, Mrs Richards, but like all the girls I have a very soft spot for Mystery Miguelito at Pepe's. I suppose all the British girls fall for Spaniards at first — because they're so handsome and vital and have such a love of living.'

The old woman wagged her finger. 'Don't make it sound so unlikely. Your Miguelito has to fall in love himself one day. It might be you.'

'After hearing your story, I suppose I do have a chance. But it's so different with me. You see, I'm only in love with a fantasy figure. I don't know Miguelito—I've never met him to speak to.'

'Would you like to meet him?'

'Oh, yes—if only to tell him what pleasure his music and his guitar have brought me.' Shelley looked at her watch. 'My goodness, I've made you talk for far too long. Come and lie down now, and have a rest before dinner.'

She helped the old lady to her bed. Mrs Richards said thoughtfully, 'You aren't afraid of close relationships, are you?'

Shelley felt herself blush hotly. 'No.'

'Because sometimes girls who get crushes on singers do so because they pose no physical threat. . .'

'Some do, I'm sure of it. Now close your eyes, my dear, and sleep a little.'

Shelley walked back to the reception-room. Victoria wasn't there—she would have gone home by now. Consuelo had not yet arrived. But Miguel Rafaelo sat at the desk, looking through the files that Shelley had made of all the patients she had seen. He looked as though he had been there for some time, and Shelley had a funny feeling that he was looking studiously down to hide the fact that he had been listening at the door to her conversation with Mrs Richards.

But he looked up and smiled quite normally, and she didn't have the nerve to ask him if he had been listening. He pushed across a small phial and a bottle of tablets. 'I think you were looking for these?'

'They're the ones missing from the drug cupboard?' She picked them up, and nodded. 'Yes, these are definitely the ones I couldn't find.' She asked, 'Were they found in someone's apartment?'

'No, Shelley, and I'm glad to tell you their removal was nothing at all to do with you. Consuelo had taken them out to get at the anti-inflammatory tablets for the patient with the sprained ankle. She had taken them out so that she could read the labels on the other bottles—and for super-safe keeping she had locked them in my drawer while she went through all the tablets looking for the ones she wanted. She has apologised, of course, but I don't blame her—she wasn't used to working here, and she had erred on the side of safety, so all is well, and you, Shelley, had done nothing wrong. You had locked the door after treating Mrs Richards, with all the drugs in their correct places. Panic over!'

'I'm very relieved.'

'She will be here soon. Don't make her feel uncomfortable about it, will you?'

'You know I won't.'

'Yes—I know.' His voice was neutral. 'You—have caught up with your sleep after the weekend?'

'Yes, thank you.'

'I hope we have a quiet week. Mrs Richards can go home if she wishes tomorrow. It would be an idea to get a girl from the village to look after her at home for two or three weeks. I'm sure there must be someone who would be glad of the money.'

Shelley said eagerly, 'I think I know just the person.'

'Who?'

'Dolores Freitas's daughter.'

'Young Lina? But she's pregnant.'

'She's young and healthy. Mrs Richards only needs someone to sit with her and bring her newspapers and her knitting, doesn't she?'

'Yes. She can have her meals sent from the café. What made you think of Lina?'

Shelley still wasn't sure how much of her conversation with Mrs Richards Miguel had overheard, so she said, 'You were listening to us chatting earlier?'

'I heard your voices, but I wasn't listening.'

Shelley said, 'I think they'll get on well.' She was just trying to find the right words to explain why she thought Mrs Richards would enjoy meeting Abuelo Freitas's granddaughter, when Consuelo arrived to take over the evening shift, and the conversation switched to other matters.

After a while Miguel said, 'Right—well, I'll leave you to it. Shelley, you've been here all day. Go and relax a little.'

'I will, but would you do that favour for Mrs Richards? Ask Lina if she'd like to come up and help out for a few weeks? You'll be going that way, won't you?'

'Yes, of course.'

Just then Victoria popped her head in. She was dressed in black, and was wearing rather a lot of make-up. 'I've brought the Mercedes, Miguel. Are you ready? I'm dying to see what you've got for me tonight!'

'You're always dying for something, girl. Last time it was to see the new designs at the boutique. Did you buy anything that day, by the way?'

'I did—a super sweater threaded with gold, and an apricot-pink body suit. I put it on your bill.'

Miguel's face was boyishly animated. 'What a woman! Will you never grow up, Victoria?'

'I hope not. I don't want to be old and stuffy like you! Come on, Miguel. You've already stayed much later than you said.'

'Coming, coming. Some of us old people have certain responsibilities, you know—like patients.'

'I know. I'm sorry. But I know Mrs Richards is doing very well, and she'll be absolutely fine with Consuelo here.'

'Sure, sure.' Miguel smiled at Consuelo and Shelley. 'I'll say goodnight, then. Have a peaceful time.'

Shelley nodded, and said, 'You're taking your phone?'

'Yes, Shelley, I have it here.'

'And you won't forget about asking Lina?'

'I promise. Victoria, remind me to stop at the Freitases' house as we go through the village.'

They finally left, with Consuelo unable to stop herself from running to the door when she heard the sound of a big, powerful expensive engine being started. She came back with a large smile. 'What a limousine, Shelley!'

'A Mercedes? Yes, I heard what Victoria said.' Shelley wasn't moved by motor cars, especially while her mind was working out where Miguel was taking Victoria, and why he was footing her dress bills. But Consuelo seemed to want a little more enthusiasm, so she added, 'He's not a poor man. Why shouldn't he own a limousine?'

'He deserves it,' agreed Consuelo. 'He gives jobs to all the people in Santa Barbara, and he looks after their health also. He is a good man.'

'He needs someone to help him with that estate.'

Consuelo agreed. 'There was a lady once came to his house. I think she came from Madrid University — she was also a doctor. She is gone now to the United States to be a specialist. They say in the village that she took Miguel's soul with her.'

Shelley felt a pang of grief for the lonely man. 'She was beautiful, I suppose?'

'Not very. She had pretty hair — she was small and sharp-eyed. But she had no heart, that I know — and no soul but Miguel's. Only the brains to do the operations. No time for his fields and groves and his people.'

'So maybe Victoria will fill her place?'

Consuelo shrugged. 'Victoria is very young for him. And she also has no time for farm people, I think. We will see.'

'You make it sound as though life is passing him by.'

'Time is passing always, Shelley — tick, tick, tick — can you hear how fast away it goes?'

'Oh, don't, Consuelo, you make me feel ancient!'

The village woman laughed a hearty laugh. 'Then do something to feel young again. Take a lover, dance the flamenco, shake the castanets, buy a pink body suit!'

'I'll do all those things, Consuelo—one of these days. Just now I feel like a long cool drink and a large Knickerbocker Glory!'

'That will do for now! Forget the lover until tomorrow!'

'Or until Saturday, when I see my lovely Miguelito!' Shelley ran out lightly, her cheerfulness quite restored by the even-tempered Consuelo. But as she strolled in the evening darkness down the steps towards the restaurant where she used to meet Rosie for ice-cream, she felt the recent conversations replaying in her mind. Poor Mrs Richards and her Felipe. Poor Miguel and his lady doctor. Time was indeed passing by. . .

Lina Freitas came to the medical centre next morning. Shelley was there on her own, seeing to a couple of minor injuries while Mrs Richards dozed in the sick-room. Shelley finished binding up an infected mosquito bite, and gave the name of an anti-histamine cream that the other patient could buy from Rosie's shop.

After the patients had gone, Lina said, 'Dr Rafaelo, he say you find work for me.'

'Did he tell you I need someone to look after an old lady?'

'Yes, she have a heart attack.'

'She's better now, but rather weak. She just needs someone with her until she gets stronger.'

'That I can do very well, Señorita Shelley—I look after my *abuelito* all the time. I know old people. I listen to their stories, and I know when to let them sleep in the shade.' Lina was a pretty girl, with a totally natural smile and tangled dark curls. The priest was trying to make her marry her baby's father, the good-looking young Pablo, but Lina was in no hurry.

'Then let's go and talk to the *señora*, and see if she likes you to work for her, Lina.'

The two women went through into the sickroom, where Mrs Richards was dozing in her chair, the gentle breeze stirring her wispy white hair. Lina went straight up to her as she opened her eyes, and said, '*Señora*, I am Lina. What is your name?'

'*Hola*, Lina. I'm Señora Richards.'

'Is that what I call you?'

Mrs Richards seemed taken with the girl. 'You can call me just whatever you think suits me. Auntie, maybe?'

'What is your Christian name, *señora*?'

Shelley stared. No one ever used Mrs Richards's first name. No one knew it — although it must be on her medical records somewhere. But the old lady was smiling at the question. 'It isn't a pretty name like yours. It's just Constance.'

'Constanza — that is strange. My *abuelito* tells me I must call my baby Constanza if it is a girl.'

Mrs Richards started when the girl mentioned her grandfather. She turned to Shelley, who deliberately didn't meet her gaze. With quavering voice, she turned back to Lina. 'Lina, what is your second name?'

'Freitas.'

'Ah.' The old lady clutched at her chest for a moment, and Lina took a step forward, but Mrs Richards waved her away. 'I'm all right. Your grandmother, Lina, how is she?'

'*Abuela* died seven, eight years.'

Shelley went to her, but the old lady shook her head. 'I'm all right. . .' But her voice was faint. 'Lina, wait outside, please.'

'Yes, Señora Constanza.' Brisk and obedient, Lina had already decided what she would call her new mistress.

When she had left the room, the old lady said, 'Oh, Shelley, that was a naughty trick to play on me. It's Felipe's granddaughter, and you guessed it.'

'But his wife is dead, Mrs Richards. What harm can there be in making friends with his family? Through Lina? You are a neighbour, after all, and you love the place. What can be wrong in making friends?'

'Pain, Shelley dear, pain, pain, pain. The wasted life and the wasted love that comes to me in the night and makes me cry out in pain.' Mrs Richards reached out and took Shelley's hand, holding it so tightly that the nails dug into Shelley's skin. 'Send her away, Shelley. Send her away now. I don't want to see her again.'

'Very well.' Shelley went through to Lina, but she didn't dismiss her. Instead, she dug into her own pocket and said, 'Mrs Richards doesn't need any help today, Lina, but here's some money in advance, and someone will come to fetch you when she's ready to go back to her villa.'

'*Sí*—OK, I go now. Maybe next time I bring her some oranges from the best side of the orchard—very sweet, and will do her lot of good. I bring for you too, Señorita Shelley.' Lina waved cheerfully, as she set off back to the village of Santa Barbara. Shelley watched her. If anyone could melt Mrs Richards's pain, it was this child. But Shelley knew she couldn't rush things after a lifetime of mistakes.

'I said she might come and visit you—she wanted to bring you some oranges to bring the colour back to your cheeks.'

Mrs Richards pretended to sleep, but Shelley could tell by the tightly closed eyes and the hard lines at the corners of her mouth that she was shutting out the world because it was hurting again. 'You can be wise with my troubles, but not with your own,' she whispered. Shelley bent and stroked the hair from her patient's eyes, and left her in peace. Maybe the squabbling sparrows on the next balcony would talk some sense into her before it was too late.

* * *

The week had gone quickly because she had been busy. Miguel came in on Friday evening, after seeing very little of the medical centre that week. 'You still have Mrs Richards here?' he asked.

'Yes. I thought she might stay until next week. She's doing no harm here, and I'm company for her.'

'She sent Lina away, then?'

'Yes.'

'Are you going to tell me why?'

'Only if you order me. I think it was told to me in confidence.'

'Does it concern the Frietas family in some way?'

'In some slight way, yes.'

Miguel saw that he was getting nowhere, and gave up on that topic. 'Well, Shelley, I told Consuelo not to come because I thought Mrs Richards would be back in her villa.'

'No problem.'

Another voice broke in—Constance Richards's. 'No problem, exactly, Doctor. I would not dream of staying here and making Shelley stay just because of me. I am going home. Please have my things sent along. I can manage very nicely by myself.'

It was no use Shelley protesting. The old lady would have walked back to her villa, but Miguel stopped her by closing the door, and insisting that she wait for a golf cart. 'And I want to come in with you, and make sure you have everything you need.'

'I have a chambermaid each morning, and I'll tell her if I need anything. You can stay here and take Shelley out to dinner. She's worked very hard and I'm a difficult patient. She deserves a treat.'

'No, please—I'm not hungry.' Shelley was unwilling to be alone with Miguel, in case his gentle conversation got through to her, and uncovered her sensitivity that she tried so hard to hide.

'I'm not doing anything,' he said mildly, 'if you change your mind.'

She thought of what Consuelo had said about the lady doctor who had taken Miguel's soul. He might be lonely tonight, and actually welcome her company. But no, not after seeing Victoria riding away in that Mercedes, after putting her clothes purchases on Miguel's bill... Of course she had suspected there was something between them, when Victoria had questioned her so closely. But that evening was decisive. The nurses in the Monte Samana clinic were only temporary pastimes, and Shelley was just number four.

Shelley said quietly, 'I mean it—I couldn't eat anything tonight.'

'You're getting thinner. You aren't dieting, are you?' He seemed anxious about her.

'Oh, not you too! There was Mrs Richards telling me I ought to take vitamins. And Lina, offering me oranges for their health-giving properties. What is this? A be-kind-to-Shelley week?'

The golf cart arrived, and Miguel helped Mrs Richards into it. She refused to let him come with her, but reluctantly agreed that either he or Shelley could call and see her every day before she went out or undertook any exercise other than gentle walking. He watched the little electric cart trundle away, then he turned and took Shelley's hand. 'Come out with me tonight, Shelley, and I'll take you to meet Miguelito tomorrow.' His name exploded in her mind, but she did her best to remain calm.

'You mean it?'

'It's time you two got together.' He waited, and she saw a hint of amusement in his face. She found herself wondering how often he thought of his lady friend in America, and feeling sorry for a man who could be such fun, but who spent so much of his time working. He said, 'I can hear your mind working, Shelley.'

'You're blackmailing me, of course—you realise that, don't you? Blackmail is a crime.' She was stalling for time. Meet Miguelito!

He smiled and shrugged. 'OK, then, if you want me to play it straight, I'll introduce you tomorrow whether you come out for dinner with me tonight or not.'

'Where will we meet him? It won't be much fun if it's just a brief handshake in the middle of Pepe's dance-floor. Maybe we could go out for a drink afterwards? Are you very friendly with him, or do you really despise him as much as you say?' And now that the meeting was so close, did she really want it?

'Hey, steady on! Are we having dinner or not?'

'Yes, all right. I must go and change, though.'

'Shall we meet by the pool in an hour?'

'All right. And Miguel—thank you.'

'It is my pleasure.' He turned, then said, looking back, 'As we're slumming tomorrow, let's go somewhere really special tonight, shall we?'

'Why?'

'You haven't seen much of Cartagena—you've been working too hard. I think we could both do with a luxury evening with good food, soft lights and a tranquil background. And an early night too. What do you say? Got any glad rags that would fit the bill?'

Shelley was silent. When Miguel tipped her chin so that she had to look into his eyes, she said rather bitterly, 'It sounds rather like where you took Victoria in the Mercedes, Miguel. I'm afraid I don't run to pink body suits—and the jeep is quite glamorous enough for me.'

'Oops! Your eyes are turning green, Shelley. I was only taking Victoria to meet her——' He stopped, then his voice changed. 'To meet her couturier at the Hilton. I promise we won't go anywhere near there!'

'Good.'

'See you in an hour, then? No overdressing?'

'All right. And I wasn't jealous of Victoria, you know—just expressing a preference for a less flamboyant evening.'

'Sure.' He reached out casually as she turned to go,

and caught her hand in his, letting it slip very gradually away from his fingers as she moved back. It was a gesture that touched her, and as she walked away along the fragrant walkway towards the road up to Rosie's villa she looked at her fingers in the moonlight, and found herself smiling.

Rosie was lounging on the couch in an orange silk shirt-dress, drinking cola from a can while Francisco sorted through the stack of CD discs. 'We're going to the Casablanca Club tonight, Shelley. Would you like to come along? It's good fun.'

'I'm meeting Miguel.'

'You don't sound very enthusiastic!'

She told her secret. 'He's finally promised to introduce me to Mystery Miguel tomorrow. The least I could do was agree to have dinner with him.'

Francisco said, 'Don't you like Dr Rafaelo? He's a popular guy around the complex. The best of the management bunch, that's for sure.'

'I do like him, yes.' But he had to be kept at arm's length, because of Victoria, and because of the other three nurses. And because of Miguelito. . .

Miguel drove her—in the jeep—to the nearest fishing port, and they dined simply on paella and lager. He was quiet, waiting for Shelley to talk, and she began to feel sorry because she hadn't been impressed by his offer of a swish night out. She said, 'I'm not good company—I'm sorry. I should have let you choose where to go. I like it here, but I can see you aren't enjoying yourself.'

'Yes, I am. I'm with you, for a start, and I happen to like being with you. You're honest and you're warm and kind. And of course, as I told you long ago, you are beautiful, and I like the looks I get from other men when I'm with a beautiful woman.'

Shelley didn't contradict him when he said that. At one time it would have embarrassed her. Tonight she said thoughtfully, 'The other nurses who worked for you—were they beautiful too?'

'I thought them not too bad at the time. But that was before I met you.'

'Oh, Miguel, you say these things in such a serious voice that I do almost believe you. Did you make love to these other women?'

'Does it matter?'

'I was told that you broke their hearts.'

'That doesn't really make sense. I made no promises to them. I didn't try to make them fall for me, because at that time I wasn't in the mood for that sort of thing.'

'I see.'

'Do you?'

'Yes, Miguel, I think so. There was someone special——'

'Who said so? Victoria? I told her never——'

'Not Victoria, someone from Santa Barbara. They all knew. I don't want you to talk about her if it hurts. I only want you to know I understand.'

They walked along by the harbour, where the tall masts and the draped fishing nets made a dramatic backcloth as the men prepared for their nightly trip out, working on the nets and the sailing gear by the light of lanterns, and with much singing and swearing and good-natured banter.

They stopped at the end of the harbour wall, and Miguel gently drew Shelley against him, so that they walked back linked together. He admitted quietly, 'I was very sad for a long time, but not now. I realise now that she didn't have the qualities of insight and gentleness and the warmth she would need to be the companion of a country doctor.'

'Even if he is a tycoon in his spare time?'

'Even if.' He kissed her, without undue passion, and, despite herself, Shelley reached up her arms and held him close. The embrace went on for a long time, but Miguel kept his self-control, so that their kisses, although they grew sweeter and more languid, never became threatening.

In the jeep, he drove with one hand, putting the other over hers on her knee. He drove her right to the door of the villa. Switching the engine off, he leaned over and kissed her again, and this time she was waiting for him, kissing him back with an inner longing. As he drew back and wished her goodnight, she saw a gleam of amusement in his eyes, before he put his glasses on again. She touched his hand. 'What's amusing you?' she asked.

He smiled, and put his hand against her cheek, smoothing it gently. 'Shelley, you're beautiful,' he said.

CHAPTER SEVEN

SHELLEY woke with a feeling of destiny. Rosie came into her room with a mug of coffee, and sat on the bed. 'It isn't everyone who gets to meet their Prince Charming.'

That was just what Shelley was thinking, but she tried to play down her excitement. 'He probably won't turn up.'

'That's rather negative, isn't it?'

'I hope you haven't told anyone.'

'No. Who would believe me anyway? Miguelito has been singing at Pepe's Bar for years. Why should he suddenly grant you an audience? What have you got that thousands haven't?'

Shelley grinned. 'Friends in high places?'

'If you ask me, Miguel Rafaelo is falling for you.'

Shelley was thoughtful for a moment, then she changed the subject. 'He doesn't know, you know—Miguelito doesn't know that he's going to be unmasked tonight. It hasn't been arranged. Miguel's going to ask him on the night—out of the blue. He might refuse. In fact, now that I think over what you just said, I'm sure he'll refuse. Dr Rafaelo's an important man in Monte Samana, but he has no clout in Pepe's Bar. Miguelito's bound to say no to meeting a fan.'

'That's probably true, Shelley. He gets paid by Pepe, not by the complex. He doesn't have to do what Miguel Rafaelo wants.'

Shelley sipped her coffee, then put the mug down and swung her legs on to the cool tiled floor. 'Well, now that we've decided that nothing is going to happen tonight that doesn't happen every Saturday night in

Pepe's Bar, tell me — why on earth can you even think for a second that Miguel is falling for me?'

'I don't know. You just seem — right together. Do you still think he's stuffy and old-fashioned?'

'No, I don't. He's very nice, in fact. But I'm not going to be number four, all the same. We're just good friends — just colleagues.'

'You like him, don't you?'

'Of course I like him. He's one of the nicest men I've ever met in my life. But it doesn't mean I'm potty about him.'

'You're getting angry. I must have touched on a sensitive spot.'

'Rosie, I have no sensitive spots. I'm psychoanalysed. No more problems.'

Her friend's face wrinkled in one of her famous chuckles. 'You're giving up men, then? That's the only way to keep life uncomplicated — give up men.'

Shelley thought about that one. 'I don't think I could do that. Just because there are men like Ken Noakes around, it doesn't mean that they're all bad.'

Rosie jumped up and went to the wardrobe. 'Come on, then, let's decide what you're wearing for your presentation to the king.'

Shelley followed her. 'I wonder if Miguel knows what his favourite colour is?'

The bed was strewn with dresses, skirts and blouses when the telephone rang. Shelley ran to answer it. It must be the medical centre. '*Hola?*'

'*Hola*, Shelley — good that you are in. Victoria here. A boy has come off his motor-cycle at the roundabout outside the main gates. Instead of taking him straight to hospital, the gatekeeper has him brought up here. Will you come and take a look? He says he isn't badly hurt, and doesn't want to go all the way to hospital.'

'Of course. I'll be five minutes.' Shelley hastily pulled on a pair of jeans and a thin cotton sweater, and stuck her feet into sandals. 'Duty calls, Rosie. Leave me a note if I miss you later.'

'You won't need me. Dr Rafaelo to escort you, and the dishy Miguelito to bring you home. I bet he's a passionate type—all hot-blooded and Spanish and macho!'

From the door Shelley shouted, 'I thought we'd decided he wouldn't agree to meet me!' And she didn't wait for a reply.

Victoria was chatting to the patient, a good-looking raven-haired youth with the dark eyebrows and flashing black eyes of the typical Andalusian. He lay on the examination couch, and his left cheek was badly grazed down one side. Victoria looked up, and her face was flushed and animated. Yes, Shelley could see why— the young man undoubtedly wasn't too ill to pay compliments. Shelley said, smiling and coming up to take his pulse, 'Well, *señor*, what have you been doing to our road? Did you know there's a penalty for digging holes in it with your face?'

Victoria said defensively, 'That roundabout is terribly dangerous, you know, Shelley. Modesto wasn't speeding. The angle is too sharp——'

'When you're going too fast,' said Shelley. 'But I'm not here to make judgements, only to see if you've broken anything. You can tell me the day and the month? And your name and address? And the name of the King? Good, good.' There seemed no neurological deficit. She tested his reflexes carefully, and felt his limbs and joints for damage. 'You fell on your head?'

'Head and shoulder. I was wearing a helmet, but it was ripped off as I skidded across the road.'

She examined the shoulder again, and made him sit up while she tested the arm for full movement. He didn't cry out, but she saw him wince. 'Modesto, I don't think you've broken your collarbone, but you're badly bruised. If I had my way I'd X-ray just to make sure. But even if it is broken, the treatment will be the same. Immobilise the joint for a while and keep the arm in a sling.'

'I can do without going to the hospital? Only I am — meeting someone——'

'Yes, of course you are—it's Saturday, isn't it!' Shelley teased him. 'And you want someone to send a message to the young lady to explain why you're late?'

Sheepishly he nodded, 'Yes, please.'

Victoria said, 'I have my car, Shelley. Shall I take him home?'

'What a kind thought. All right, I'll put a sling on that arm, and if the pain gets worse you must promise to take yourself to the hospital.'

'I will, I promise. Thank you, thank you, *señorita*, you are both very kind to me.'

'It's a good job you're young and healthy,' said Shelley. 'But stay off that bike until the shoulder's properly healed.'

Victoria lent him her shoulder to lean on, a situation which they both seemed to find highly agreeable. As he limped out, his good arm clinging on to Victoria's shapely waist, Shelley called after them, 'And mind the roundabout! Drive slowly, Victoria.'

'I always do. I told you, I know how dangerous those sharp bends are!'

Shelley went to Reception. 'I'll be in the pool until later, then in the villa for a siesta.'

'I think I know where you will be tonight!' laughed the girl.

Shelley felt herself blushing. She had made no secret of her admiration for the mysterious Miguelito. But that was before—when he was a distant, glamorous idol for the masses to worship. If she really did meet him, how many people would know about it? No, surely he would swear her to secrecy—if he really did agree in the end to Miguel's request.

She hesitated by the telephone, then dialled

Miguel's home number. He could be out on the patio, or walking among his lemon groves. If he didn't answer after three rings, she would put it down. But he did answer, almost at once. '*Hola? Rafaelo aquí.*'

'Hello, Miguel. Shelley.'

'I could not mistake that voice. How are you, Shelley? Not an emergency?'

'No, nothing to do with work. I'm ringing to tell you not to—not to go ahead tonight. I don't want to meet Miguelito—I've changed my mind. You didn't mean it anyway, did you? You were testing me out, to see if— if I'd stopped being timid with men, isn't that it?'

She could tell he was smiling as he replied. 'The thought never crossed my mind.'

'You're lying, but never mind. Just don't ask him to meet me, OK?'

'I already have, Shelley—sorry. But I'll call him and cancel it, if you insist.'

'He agreed?' Her voice seemed to grow small suddenly.

'For me, he agreed—but only for a moment, and in the dark.'

'Oh.' Shelley thought for a moment. 'What did you tell him about me?'

'What I know. That you are British, blonde and pretty and clever, and you work with me in the medical centre. He said he has noticed you.'

Her voice was even smaller. 'And he's going to come and say hello?'

'That's right. But I think I can get him at home if you want to call it off.'

'No!' That would make things worse. Better get it over with, then. 'No, don't do that. Now that it's fixed, we might as well go ahead. I'm not scared or anything, Miguel—that's not why I rang. It's just that it seems a pity for him to reveal his identity. It's part of the act, his mystery, and I don't want to be the one to ruin it.'

'That's very thoughtful of you, Shelley. He would

appreciate that. But I told him you wouldn't tell a soul.'

'Oh,' said Shelley again. 'I've already told Rosie, and she's probably told Francisco and Carlos.'

'That's tough. You'll have to lie to them, afterwards, and say he didn't show up.'

'Yes, that's what I'll do.'

'Good. Then it's all arranged. What time shall I pick you up?'

'Whatever is a suitable time for you.'

'Where are you ringing from, by the way?'

'The medical centre.' She explained about the motor-cyclist. 'Victoria has taken him home.'

'That explains why she didn't show up — I'd arranged to take her riding. She'll be late, then?'

'Judging by the handsomeness of the patient, I would say so,' said Shelley, with a little mild sarcasm.

Miguel didn't seem to notice it. 'I knew there would be trouble at that roundabout — the road approaches it at a very acute angle. Thank goodness it was nothing more serious. OK, Shelley, enjoy your day, and I'll be ready when you are.'

The sun was growing very hot, and the pool was the only place to be that day. The two girls swam until they were tired, then lazed on beach towels on the grass under the palm trees. Carlos and Francisco chatted to them for a while, but then Carlos had to patrol his area, which to him meant strolling around, able to approach and compliment all the prettiest girls, and subsequently trying to fit them into his tight evening schedule! Shelley said lazily, 'You didn't tell Francisco about Miguelito, did you?'

'I didn't tell anyone, Shelley. I thought it might hurt the boys' feelings if I told them we think Miguelito is better-looking than they are.'

'Good. Keep it like that.' One worry had faded, but she still wished she had never agreed to this charade. Still, Miguel would be with her. A quick handshake, and a heartfelt tribute to the beauty of his voice, and she could call it a day and go home gracefully.

Miguel's jeep was outside the villa when Shelley happened to look out. She ran out in the darkness. 'Why didn't you ring the bell? Come in, Miguel, I'm not ready yet.'

'I thought you would be eagerly waiting to meet your hero.'

'Don't be ridiculous. I'll be five minutes.' She wasn't going to let Miguel know how anxious she was to choose the right thing to wear—fashionable yet not forward, pretty but not overdressed. In the end she wore a simple white flared skirt and a broderie anglaise blouse, and left her fair hair loose on her shoulders.

'*Que linda!*' How pretty. Miguel had been sitting on the balcony staring out across the valley. The sound of the girl singer by the pool wafted up in this natural amphitheatre, and a nightingale was trilling in the branches of a casuarina in the garden. Now he came towards her with his hands outstretched. His eyes behind the glasses were deep and expressive and appreciative. He bent and kissed her cheek in a friendly, brotherly way. 'The man will be a fool if he does not immediately fall in love with you.'

'Don't talk complete nonsense, please, Miguel!'

'Even superheroes are susceptible to beauty, Shelley!'

'Oh, don't tease.'

'I think I'm jealous.'

'How can you be jealous? You eat British nurses for breakfast. I'm just the one that got away.'

They went on with this banter as they drove down the hill and along the road to the beach. Pepe's Bar was situated on the sand, with rough wooden flooring that Shelley used to think couldn't take much more of the stamping that it got each Saturday during the flamenco dancing. They went in, Miguel's arm protectively round her waist to prevent them being separated by the throng of hot, energetic dancers. 'You'd like a stiff drink?'

'Watermelon juice, please.'

'You can face Don Juan on watermelon juice?'

'Of course. I'm only going to shake hands anyway, then you can take me home.'

'No way—I've got a date. Miguelito is taking you home.'

Her voice rose considerably. 'You've what?' Several people turned to look, in spite of the loud throbbing disco music. Miguel said calmly, 'I am meeting someone else.'

'That's not fair.'

'I'm sorry, but I cannot be at your beck and call all the time, my dear. Don't forget we are only business acquaintances.'

'I know that!' It did sound rather distant, though. 'But I didn't think you would ditch me. My opinion of you has gone down, Miguel, I'm afraid. That's certainly not gentlemanly.'

He smiled and pulled her closer, and they stood with his arm around her, and her head rather comfortably on his shoulder. 'Now you know I wouldn't leave you unless I knew you were going to be all right. He'll see you home, and you can get to know one another. OK?'

'No. I'll have that drink, please.'

'Rum and Coke? Double brandy?'

'White wine, please.'

'White wine it is. Do you want to dance?'

'Yes. You've never danced with me before.'

'It's turning into quite an evening for you, isn't it? You get to dance with me, as well as meet Superman!' He was laughing at her, yet in such a nice way that she had to give in and join in the laughter. His eyes shone with mischief, and she wondered how she could ever have thought him boring. Like good wine, she thought, he improved with keeping. But even while she joked with him, she remembered those other nurses who had worked with him. For all she knew, they could have come to Pepe's with him, just as Shelley was doing tonight. The difference was that those other poor girls had allowed themselves to fall for this boyish charm, whereas Shelley was forewarned, and proof against those smiling black eyes. And when they seemed too beguiling, all she had to do was think of Victoria, and Victoria's dress account, and Victoria riding with him, and the woman he was meeting tonight—ten to one that was Victoria too.

As midnight approached, Shelley felt a fluttering in her stomach over which she had absolutely no control. She tried not to worry, but the thought of coming face to face with the handsome, the dashing Miguelito made her heart thump in her chest. 'Want to sit down?' asked Miguel.

'Yes, please.'

'Near the front?'

'Not tonight. At the back.'

'But—'

'Please?'

He nodded, and squeezed her hand as he led the way to a table. 'Now don't worry. You're going to enjoy tonight, and I'm glad for you. He doesn't speak English, by the way, but I'm sure you'll get on fine.'

She looked up at him, and said with trepidation, 'You know, this is the first time I've actually hoped there would be an urgent call from the medical centre.'

He laughed, and patted her shoulder. 'You won't be saying that tomorrow.'

And then the hubbub began to quieten down, and Shelley knew the church clock must be striking midnight. She turned to the doorway where she knew the singer would emerge as the stroke of twelve died away on the still night. She reached for Miguel's hand, but he must have moved back and she couldn't feel him near her. The bead curtain beside the bar moved, and Miguelito came through, waving both arms above his head, the guitar slung around his neck. He was wearing a white T-shirt, which showed off his perfect torso and rippling arm muscles, and his hair was loose and fashionably untidy round his handsome face, that face that was always in shadow. Shelley stared, as the old magic started up, and she felt as she had always felt when she looked at him, that all other men she knew paled into insignificance beside this one.

He smiled all round, acknowledging the applause, and kissed his hand to some of the girls at the front. Then he looked up towards the back, and Shelley knew, with a sudden shock, that he must be looking for her, but she was too nervous to stand up. Her palms were sweating, and she hoped they would stop when she had to shake hands with him. He was strumming a few chords now, one foot up on a stool, and the silence in the little bar was complete.

The song he sang was lilting and romantic and a little sad, and the voice was as thrilling as ever. Slowly she began to lose her fear, and just listen to the beauty of his music. Miguel Rafaelo was right — she had been uptight, nervous of men and afraid of the hurt they could do to her feelings. But if anyone could relax her, it was Miguelito, if in real life he was as tender, as passionate and as exciting as the music he made. Now she didn't regret agreeing to a meeting. If she had let this chance slip, she knew she would regret it for the rest of her life. And she thought for a moment of little Mrs Richards, and the regrets she had lived with for fifty years.

She turned to smile at Miguel, but he wasn't there. His date must have turned up. Shelley shrugged, and turned her attention back to the tall figure in the centre of attention. And she stood up as the song ended, clapping with all her might. Miguelito looked across at her and smiled, the white teeth showing in the darkness, even without a spotlight. She felt that she knew him already.

Then the flamenco started, and Miguelito sang with a passion and a living flame, fire and ice, desire and weeping, a throbbing sob in his voice pulsing through the building. If this man had another career it must be as a professional singer. He could coax tears and laughter and desire from his audience with a simple note, a gesture, a glance. Shelley stood bewitched, until the clear feminine shout from the wings and a clatter of castanets signalled the arrival of the dancers in their vivid flounces. Shelley sat down. She couldn't see Miguelito from here, but she had seen enough. Now all she had to do was wait. If he wanted to meet her, he would. If he had changed his mind, she couldn't really blame him. What was one admiring girl among so many beauties?

Nobody came to her. The song had ended, and dancing was going on again. Shelley stood and walked to the door. She hadn't really thought the famous singer would have time to spend with her, had she? It was a fantasy, as he was himself, it had always been a fantasy, and perhaps it was better to keep it so.

She started to walk back up the winding little street, away from the beach, through the tiny town and up towards the complex. The night was clear, with a few ragged clouds hanging like a stage set for *Swan Lake* behind the palm trees and the quaint little town roofs. There was no moon tonight. The noise of the music followed her up the cobbled street, getting fainter as she walked.

And then someone was running, lightly, behind her, and she heard someone say in a deep and thrilling voice, '*Señorita, espereme!*' Wait for me.

She stopped and turned. He was there, his white T-shirt unmistakable in the darkness, his wild hair even wilder with the running. He went on in Spanish, 'You are Shelley, yes?'

Her Spanish was fluent now, and she was able to find the right words. 'I'm Shelley Cameron, yes. I didn't think you would come.'

'I gave my word.' He smiled, and took her hand. Then he leaned forward and kissed her cheek, his breath lingering with his lips. 'That is how we greet beautiful women in Spain.'

She met his smile, basking in his undivided attention. 'I must be one of the lucky ones, to really get to meet you. You do know how much emotion you are the cause of back there, don't you?'

He laughed, and tucked his hand into the crook of her elbow. 'Come, we will walk back together. It is my promise and my pleasure.' And as they walked, Shelley couldn't quite believe that she was really awake, and not just dreaming of walking beside him, close to him, his strong fingers actually touching her flesh, and the warmth of his breath against her cheek. He said, 'So you like Spanish music, Shelley?'

'I like yours.'

'That is very honest, *señorita*! Thank you for the compliment. When my friend told me about you, I was looking forward to meeting you. Now, what would you like to ask me?'

'A lot of very personal things that I'm sure you don't wish to answer. Like if you are married, and what you do for a living apart from this. I know you avoid this sort of thing, so I won't be offended if you don't want to tell me.'

She didn't mind if he said nothing at all, as long as they could walk along like this under a starlit sky, arm in arm forever. But he did reply, hesitating a little over the words. 'I am not married. I am not sure if I would still sing if I had a wife, because I think marriage is a commitment to one woman, and I have no right to go and sing to all those others.'

Shelley liked him more and more. They were passing the lemon groves now, almost at the roundabout close to the gate to Monte Samana, and she could smell the ripe fruit in the warm darkness. She asked, 'How friendly are you with Miguel?'

'I like him very much. I respect him for what he has done in Santa Barbara. I am glad he came to live among the villagers, and I think they like him too.' He paused, then said, 'I think you also like him a little, yes?'

She said firmly, 'We are colleagues in work.'

'That is all?'

'I don't belong in his life, any more than I belong in yours or in anybody's. I'm just here for a few short months. I'm very glad I had the chance to meet you, you know, because you are one of the memories I have to take back with me.'

The gate of Monte Samana lay ahead. Miguelito said, 'You wish that I accompany you to your villa?' His voice was serious now. 'I will spend the night with you if you wish it. I like you very much, Shelley, but I will come only as far as you ask me to.'

She hadn't had time to work out an answer to such a question. They stopped in the flower-bordered road, and Miguelito looked down at her. They were very close. He murmured, 'I think I can read your mind. Goodnight, *señorita*, and I hope we will meet again.' And he bent his head and touched her lips with his.

Breathlessly she said, 'Do you have to go?'

'Yes,' he nodded. 'You may not think it, but I am quite a busy man. You will be all right walking alone to your house?'

'Oh, yes, it isn't far.'

He said, 'This Miguel—I think you are important to him, *señorita*.'

'Did he tell you to say that?'

'Do not be hard. It does not suit you.'

'I'm sorry. But I told you, he is nothing to me.'

'He knows of your feelings towards me, and I am only a passing stranger. I am not real, Shelley.'

'You are real. I know you now, and you can't be a stranger ever again. See, I can touch you. You *are* real.' And she reached out and stroked his hair. With a sudden exclamation, he caught her hand and pressed the palm of it to his lips. It roused her violently by its unexpectedness, and she made no protest when his arms went round her and he kissed her with a force and a recklessness that she met with equal need.

He drew his head back, but his arms were still holding her tight. In whispered Spanish he said, 'You are very beautiful, *preciosa señorita*. You have it in you to drive a man mad. You have it in you to awaken a very great love. Be careful, *señorita*, to catch that love when it comes, because it may only come to you once.'

She was breathless with the emotions his kisses had aroused in her. She said, 'Did it — come to you?'

'I hurt still inside. Do not let it happen to you also.' And he nibbled at her lips again, before catching them in another long exploratory kiss that brought her to a threshold of physical pleasure she had never before experienced. He drew back at last. 'Go now, please. Please. Let me watch to make sure you come to no harm.'

His words were so urgent that she obeyed. It was only as she rounded the corner that she remembered she hadn't thanked him for walking her home.

From among the lemon trees, the solitary figure watched the filmy scrap of white dress that was Shelley Cameron, until it vanished round the corner like a beautiful wood spirit. Then he kissed his fingers to her, and turned to run back home.

CHAPTER EIGHT

'NURSE CAMERON, there is a man in Reception who says his wife has fainted. What shall I tell him?'

Still groggy from sleep, Shelley shifted the telephone to her other hand. 'I'll come down. Can you get her into the medical centre? What time is it?'

'Seven o'clock. Breakfast time.'

'Not on a Sunday it isn't breakfast time. And not after what I've been through.' But professional training took over, as she stepped over the white skirt and blouse she had discarded on the floor, to get her jeans from the wardrobe, her eyes still refusing to open. Halfway down the road, she came to. It was a limpid, beautiful day, and she was a little bit in love.

But someone needed her, and as she broke into a run, she went over the differential diagnosis of a faint in her mind. The medical centre door was ajar, and the patient lay on the couch, a middle-aged lady with a pale face under the pink of her sunburn, and shallow, laboured breathing. The husband hovered. 'She took her insulin as usual before breakfast,' he told Shelley.

'Ah, diabetic!' The diagnosis was almost certain. 'Then a shot of glucose should do the trick. Did she have any warning of this collapse?'

'I don't know,' admitted the husband sheepishly. 'I had a skinful last night. I'm still groggy.'

'Did your wife also have a — er — skinful?'

'A little more than she usually does. Well, you do when you're on holiday, don't you?'

'Not if you have a medical condition,' said Shelley through gritted teeth, as she injected the fluid into the patient's arm. Within moments, the eyelids flicked open, and the woman was talking normally and trying to sit up. Shelley warned her, 'I'd advise you to stay here for a while until you feel stronger.' She took the blood-pressure and listened to the heartbeat. 'Lie back for an hour, and let your hungover husband bring you a bite of breakfast.'

She left them both smiling, with instructions to call her at once if there was any change. She wanted to go back to bed to hug inside herself lovely warm memories of last night, of the fantastic Miguelito's gentle voice and wisdom, his unforgettable kisses, and his strong dependability. What a man, what a marvellous man.

'What are you doing, sitting out there with a silly vacant grin on your face? Where's breakfast? Haven't you even put some coffee on?'

Shelley smiled enigmatically. 'Good morning, Rosie.'

Rosie stood there in a very short nightie, her hair rumpled and her eyes narrowed against the morning sunlight. 'Don't tell me — you did meet him!'

Miguelito hadn't told her to keep her experiences to herself, but somehow she knew she must. He had spoken to her in confidence, he had spoken personally and emotionally, and it would not be right to tell anyone, not even Rosie, what he had said. So she said in as offhand a voice as she could manage, 'I met him — briefly. We shook hands, and he said he liked singing. Oh, yes, and he liked Miguel Rafaelo. That's about it, really.'

'And what did you say to him?'

'That I liked his music — and that I didn't like Miguel Rafaelo as much as he did.'

'Well, that must have been a bundle of laughs. A real little orator, isn't he!'

Shelley was superior. 'Rosie, dear, last night was an experience. I wouldn't have missed meeting him for anything. Because now I know there's nothing behind the fancy shirt that interests me in the slightest.'

'Oh, how disappointing. He didn't even kiss you goodnight, then?'

Shelley wasn't a good liar. 'A brotherly peck on the cheek.'

'And I'm Sophia Loren!' Rosie saw through her friend. But she also saw something in Shelley's face, and she went on more quietly, 'OK, OK, tell me when you want to—if you want to. I won't ask any more questions.'

'Thank you, Rosie. It's just that—well, you know this isn't supposed to have happened. Miguelito just never ever meets his fans. I won't be in Santa Barbara for ever, and I don't want to mess things up for him.'

'You're right, of course. Lucky devil.' And Rosie took herself off to get dressed.

Shelley went out and sat on the balcony by herself, just drinking in the wooded hillsides beneath the clear blue sky, and grazing goats, and the tinkling of cowbells. She knew it was nothing—that she would probably not speak to Miguelito again. Even after just one evening's conversation, he had restored her faith in men—it was possible to be handsome and talented, and yet still be modest and thoughtful and courteous. His face had been hidden in the darkness, yet she thought she would recognise him if they met again. The ghost of Ken Noakes shrivelled and vanished from her subconscious. His attitude and behaviour would never bother her again.

And then Miguel Rafaelo phoned. 'I'm going to see some patients in Santa Barbara, and I thought you'd like to come, since you took it upon yourself to interfere in the Freitas family's life.'

'I only tried to get Lina a job.'

'Would you care to come?'

'Yes, of course I would.'

'Good girl.' Even ordinary words sounded nice in his gentle accented English, and she felt pleased to have Rafaelo's approbation. 'I'll come and pick you up. In fact, I think from now on you'd better keep the jeep for yourself. You use it more than I do.'

She wondered, as she sat and waited for her boss to come for her, whether he would mention meeting Miguelito last night. She would say nothing unless he asked.

Miguel Rafaelo's conversation was all about the village surgery, and the clinics he had set up there. Last night might never have happened. He was dressed casually, in a rough cotton shirt with sleeves rolled up and workman's style trousers. Yet he still looked like an academic, or a businessman, with those thick-rimmed glasses and the glossy hair carefully sleeked back over his ears. 'You did want to come?' he asked. 'Because this isn't official work, and you're free to say no. I thought you might be interested, that's all, because you know the village people, and they seem to like you.'

'Oh, I am interested. Thanks for asking me. Sometimes I prefer Santa Barbara to Monte Samana. Real people with real jobs, not just holidaymakers out to forget what they do for a living.'

'Only sometimes?'

She smiled at him, completely at ease with this man now. 'I'm always honest with you, Miguel.'

'Sometimes you prefer Monte Samana?'

'Yes, I do. I'm only human—I love to swim and play tennis, and I've made friends there too.'

'Am I one of your friends?'

'You're teasing. I consider you my friend—although I don't know what you consider me.'

'A first-class assistant.' He kept his eyes on the road ahead. They were driving past Casa Madrid now, and there were rows of peasants picking tomatoes in his fields, and a battered truck being loaded with melons.

Shelley looked at Miguel, slightly disappointed. 'An assistant isn't a friend.'

He looked at her for a moment, and a white smile brightened his suntanned face. 'To me she is. The two are indistinguishable.'

'Thank you, Miguel.'

'Don't mention it.' He swerved the jeep to a halt in the village square, under a plane tree to keep it as cool as possible in the midday heat. She watched his forearms, strong and muscular, sweating slightly, and those capable fingers that could wield a delicate scalpel as efficiently as a ten-ton tractor. They reminded her of last night, and the feeling of walking in the moonless night with her own arm intertwined with Miguelito's. Smooth and firm it had been under her own nervous touch, and she watched Miguel's muscles, catching the sunlight as he dismounted and reached up to help her. If Miguel were holding a guitar instead of a medical bag, those arms would be very similar to Miguelito's.

'Come along,' he admonished her. 'What are you daydreaming about? There's work to be done.'

'I'm coming.' They crossed the dirt road and went into the little surgery, cool out of the direct sun. Miguel chased a chicken out of the open window, and went across to his wooden desk and makeshift filing cabinets. Shelley said, 'I thought you said you had a clinic today? There's nobody here.'

'I wanted to come early on purpose, Shelley. You see, some of your ideas are beginning to rub off on me, and I want to start keeping better records here, as well has have regular weekly clinics instead of just coming up here on a casual basis.'

'That's good. You'll have people bring their children, if they know when you'll be here. You can keep proper child-care files. I'm sure the mothers will appreciate it.'

'That's your job.'

'What is? Filing?'

'Yes. Here's the list I've made so far — all the children I have seen in the last three weeks. We'll build up until I know exactly what diseases all the kids have had, who has been vaccinated, and what home conditions are like.'

Shelley sat at the desk and took the pile of cards Miguel dumped before her from the filing cabinet. 'They aren't even in alphabetical order!'

'You don't have to do it if you don't want to.'

'I hate paperwork as a general rule, but as it's for the good of the villagers, I'll sort it out for you. I'll probably make a better job of it than you would.'

'That's true.'

'Although Victoria Sanchez would do it even better than I would.'

'No, she doesn't know enough medicine. She would spell the diseases wrong.'

'That's a weak excuse, Miguel! She's a clever girl, and quick to learn.' Shelley paused, then added, 'And she comes to visit you quite often, doesn't she?'

'Now and again. But not to work.'

'You don't mix business and pleasure?'

He wasn't sure if she was being sarcastic. but his answer was calm and equable. 'Not as a rule.'

Shelley started sorting the patients' cards into order, and wonderered why she felt a little hurt at the thought of Victoria coming and going at the Casa Madrid. It was, after all, none of Shelley's business. Miguel said, 'I'll be back in a while. I must just run up to the Casa to make sure the lorry comes back for another load. See you in an hour.'

'*Hasta luego.*' She didn't look up from her work. But he didn't move from the doorway until she did look up. 'Why are you waiting?'

His face was in shadow, his broad frame outlined against the sunshine of the little dappled square. His voice was low as he said, 'Are you going to see Miguelito again?'

'What does it matter to you?'

'It doesn't matter at all. I just wondered.'

'That's my business.'

'Ah, yes, of course it is.'

'I'm only your assistant.'

'I know, but without me you would never had had that chance.'

'I'm sorry—that's true. Thank you for what you did.'

'And?'

'You're very inquisitive. But I owe you, so yes, it was very special to me, meeting him and talking. . . I think my feelings about men in general turned from negative to positive last night.' She turned back to her work. 'Of course, all that's very personal. But I am grateful.'

'Are you seeing him again?'

'No. I'm sure he wouldn't want it. All his thing about secrecy and mystery—I wouldn't expect him to risk it again.'

'What shall I tell him when I see him?'

'Nothing. Nothing at all, Miguel. Oh, it was all just—very private, and I don't want to break his confidence.'

'Right. I understand. I'll see you in an hour.'

Shelley had straightened Miguel's appalling filing system, and was just putting all the cards back in the cabinet when the woman who kept the village shop came to the door. 'Señorita, you are open to see patients? Only I have closed the shop for siesta, and I wanted to talk to you about my husband. He isn't well, but he refuses to see the doctor.'

'Where is he now?' asked Shelley.

'He is getting the new ham out of the fridge for selling when we open at five. Señorita Shelley, I am worried. He does not eat, and he is very thin. He is afraid, I think, that he has something—incurable.'

'There's very little that is incurable these days, Inés. But he must come along and have a proper examination.'

'I can tell you his symptoms.'

'Go ahead. When did the trouble start?'

'Six months ago. His brother died of a tumour, and we went to the funeral, and since then he has not eaten well.'

'That's why he's thin.'

'I know, but how can I make him eat when he refuses?'

'He needs tests — X-rays and blood tests. Tell him the doctor is doing a survey of all the people in Santa Barbara. Dr Rafaelo will pick up anything then.'

'I'll try. Are you really doing a survey?'

'Yes, we hope to.' Shelley told her about their plans for a regular baby clinic and surveys of children and old people. 'Every week for babies. Monthly for the others.' There would be no problem passing the news around. Once they talked of it in the village shop, the whole village would know by nightfall.

Miguel had not returned. Shelley closed the filing cabinet and the desk, and wondered whether he had forgotten her. She could drive back — he had left the jeep. But it seemed polite to visit the Freitas family, especially after Lina had come to Monte Samana on a fruitless errand. Besides, Lina was an expectant mother, and Abuelo Freitas was on their list of elderly patients in need of regular visits.

The luncheon table in the little cottage was spread with cheese, olives, sardines and bread. Dolores and her father were already at the table, and her two brothers were just washing their hands in the kitchen with young Pablo the fisherman who was Lina's intended. 'Come in, please come in and share our meal,' they invited.

After much genuine persuasion, Shelley thanked them and sat down at the table. 'Is Lina all right?' Her plate was heaped with cheese, cucumber and tomatoes as they spoke.

'You do not know? The woman from Monte Samana

sent a message asking her to go today and spend some time with her. Lina was very pleased. She likes that woman.'

Shelley looked across at Abuelo, sitting in his usual place at the head of the table. His wrinkled face must once have been handsome. It was still dignified, the eyes clear and the bone-structure good. 'I'm glad my idea worked out,' she said. 'You have not met this old lady yet?'

'No, indeed. She is very rich, *no*?'

'Quite well off.'

'You would not have asked for Lina unless you liked the old lady.'

'I like her a lot. Maybe you'll meet her some day.'

The old man spoke for the first time. 'Rich people do not waste time in our village.'

'Some rich people are quite human, *señor*, I promise you!'

'Hmmph! I grant you Dr Rafaelo is more than human. He is *fantástico*. But who else?'

Shelley was longing to ask him what his first name was, but it seemed impolite, so instead she said, 'Have you never in your long life met anyone rich you liked?'

His black eyes were sharp as he looked at her and thought for a moment. 'Naturally I have liked some rich people. One meets them, in passing. But how many do you see in this village, *señorita*?'

'A good point, *señor*.'

After the meal, Dolores had cut up a huge melon, and dished out chunks on their plates. Then she brought them all strong black coffee. 'It is an honour to have you here,' she told Shelley.

'You're very kind to me.'

'How long you are staying in the complex?'

'As long as they'll have me. My present contract is for six months.'

Abuelo Freitas said, 'Dr Rafaelo wants that you stay.'

'Did he say so?'

'He does not have to say anything.'

She smiled to herself. 'If he wants me, he only has to ask. I'd love to stay on here. And he does need an assistant now that we're having regular clinics.'

Old Señor Freitas coughed, before he said, 'Sometimes *señoritas* have families who want them to go back to their own country.'

Shelley wondered if she was reading more into his comments than he actually meant. It did sound very much like the flip side to Mrs Richards' story. She said, 'I have no parents or close relatives. My work is my family. But I quite agree with you, that some young women have ties that stop them doing exactly what they wish—until it's too late, in many cases.' She watched him carefully, as he nodded in agreement.

'You have a wise tongue in your head, *señorita*.'

'That's a great compliment, Abuelo.'

Just then one of the young men said, 'Señor Felipe has seen a lot of life, *señorita*. I'm grateful that you listen to him, and do not treat him like a fool just because he is old.'

She said, 'But he's right. Young people sometimes have to make hard choices to please other people. I'm one of the lucky ones—I can choose where to live. And if Santa Barbara will have me, this is where I'd like to choose.'

Abuelo Freitas reached out and shook her by the hand. 'You can stay here as long as you like, even though you have deprived me of my oldest friend.'

'Friend, Abuelo Freitas?'

'My old pipe!'

After the laughter, they asked her to stay on, but it was siesta time, and she insisted on leaving. 'Give Lina my love,' she said.

There was no one in the glare of the sun in the village street, and the brown earth shone yellow and the dogs and chickens sought the shade. Then Shelley realised that the jeep was gone. She would have to walk back in the afternoon sunshine, or find somewhere to rest. She decided to rest, having treated enough cases of sunstroke to know very well how easily it was caught. It was thoughtless of Miguel to take the vehicle—but maybe he'd needed it in a hurry. And he didn't know where to find her to let her know.

She walked along to the little café, where at least the umbrellas and the plane trees gave some shade. From her seat she could see the winding road that led up to the elegant gateway of Casa Madrid, and she could even see the sprinklers sending blessed water swirling over the melon and pineapple fields. If she could be sure Miguel was there, she could walk up and ask for the jeep. It seemed a better idea than sitting in the village street for three hours. Shelley made up her mind, and set off to walk the quarter of a mile. At least the lemon trees gave some shade along the road.

The Casa Madrid seemed deserted. But the gates were open, and she wandered in, seeking shade. Round the back, in the patio by the pool, a table was set with the remains of lunch. The maid was there, clearing things away. '*Señorita*, I was expecting you—see, I set a place. You have eaten?'

'Yes, thank you—I ate with the Freitas family. I didn't know I was expected. The doctor didn't say.'

Miguel's voice came from the dim interior. 'You said you considered me your friend, Shelley. Don't friends visit without invitations?'

'That's exactly what I'm doing—I've come here, haven't I?'

'Would you have come for lunch?' he asked.

'I don't know. But Dolores invited me.'

The maid had cleared away, and now she came out with a jug of wine and two glasses. She smiled at Shelley before retiring. Miguel said 'Sit down, then, and share some wine with me.'

'Why didn't you come back?'

'I was hoping you would show me how friendly we were by coming to get me.'

'Oh, Miguel, that's silly—there's no need to test me out!'

'I know. I'm proud of you. You have shown me that you think my people are your brothers. You treat them with warmth and understanding. You don't know how glad I was to see you in that little cottage talking to old Freitas. Now all I have to do is persuade you to sign a contract for a lot longer than six months, and we've got ourselves a deal. Will you, Shelley?'

Smiling broadly, she said simply, 'I'd love to. It's exactly what I want. I can see now that you had to test me a little. How long a contract will you give me?'

'Drink first before negotiating.' He had poured the rosé wine into the simple tumblers, and the sun made diamonds sparkle on the surface. He held up the glass to her. 'When you work here, we can do this every afternoon! *Salud*, partner.'

Shelley hid a yawn. Miguel reached out and took her hand in his. 'Poor Shelley. Come—you've worked hard today. I'll show you where you can siesta. Then I'll take you back.'

He led her inside. The archways were all curtained to help keep out the sun. He took her to a cool shady room with a large bed, the venetian blinds closed, thin silky curtains from floor to ceiling and a fan swishing gently. 'The bathroom is through that door. Rest for a while.'

'Where will you be?'

'Here and there. Now go.' He left the room, smoothing his hair back with that gesture that was a habit with him, as though letting his hair down would literally be a bad thing. Shelley smiled after him. So Santa Barbara was her destiny after all. She had been quick to accept. Didn't she even want time to think things over? Ravished by a sunny afternoon, a pool set with palm trees and a jug of wine with a good-looking young doctor, she had agreed without even thinking of the drawbacks. Too tired to think any more, she kicked off her sandals and freshened herself up in the scented blue-tiled bathroom, brushing her hair and wiping her hands and face, and then her feet, on the fluffiest white towel she had ever felt. Then she went through and threw herself on the comfortable cool silk bedcover, and lay in luxury, gazing up at the gently rotating white fan.

When she awoke, she tried to turn, but found herself anchored by a heavy masculine arm across her waist. Turning her head, she found Miguel beside her, without his glasses, his hair awry, breathing steadily and deeply. She couldn't be annoyed—he looked so innocent and helpless in sleep. And the arm round her— could she be angry with that? It did make her feel very secure and protected, an uncommon occurrence with Shelley. After the Ken Noakes episode in her life, she had never allowed anyone to come so close to her. But it was all so different now.

She raised herself on one elbow, so that she could look down on his face. It was familiar to her now, and she knew just where his cheek curved, how his jawline made a firm outline for those tender lips, whose searching touch she knew, and had now rejected. Miguel began to stir, and opened his eyes. He smiled. For a long moment they lay and she gazed down at him, their eyes locked. Inevitably, he raised his arm and pulled her down, so that their lips met. The kiss grew stronger and wilder, and he rolled over so that he covered the length of her. She lost any sense of time, knowing only the world of sensation and pleasure and sad longing. And then the telephone rang on the little table beside them, and as Miguel rolled away to reach for it Shelley hastily rolled in the opposite direction, and sat on the edge of the bed with her back to him, smoothing back her hair and getting her breath back.

Then she heard him say in Spanish, 'You want to meet her again?'

Shelley turned, suddenly very alert. Miguel was saying 'Yes' and 'I see' while his caller did the talking. Then he said, 'OK, I'll do my best. *Adiós, amigo.*'

After he had put the phone down, he looked at his watch before the inevitable fingers pushed through his hair, forcing it back, and reached for his glasses, that magic movement that turned him back to Dr Rafaelo. He leaned back on the padded headboard and smiled at Shelley. 'Have dinner with me?'

'I think better not.'

'That was your *amigo* Miguelito on the phone. Wants to walk you home next Saturday.'

'Honestly?'

'Are you willing?'

'No, not any more. If he's really interested he can do his own asking. I'm not meeting him by appointment.'

'I don't blame you for that. Dinner?'

She was staring into space. 'Where does he live?'

'Miguelito lives — oh, around Santa Barbara.'

'And does he have a job?'

'You didn't ask him that?'

'I forgot.'

Miguel stood up and walked round to her, and said, ruffling her hair, 'He really did get to you, didn't he?'

Shelley said briskly, 'Yes — well, as I say, it's been a nice day, Miguel, and I think it's time I went home.'

'Why? Rosie isn't there. Let's go to the beach for a barbecue.'

'I don't know why, but I feel wrong staying here. I'm only your assistant ——'

'Partner!'

'Future partner, when you sort out the details.'

'So what else?'

'Well, I don't — I mean I've no right ——'

'You have as much right to be here as anyone.

Shelley, dear, stay, please! What else do you have to do? Do you really not like spending time with me? We could talk about the clinics, if you like.'

She tried to stay brisk and businesslike. 'Number four nurse doesn't want to be bad-mannered to her host, but she doesn't want to be number four casualty.'

'You won't fall for me, Shelley—not when you've got that musical muscleman ringing up about you. No, your being here is just a friendship thing, OK? Now what will it be? Beach? Fishing village? Barbecue? Or just Knickerbocker Glories back at the complex?'

Shelley couldn't help smiling at his persistence. Her boss certainly had an almost irresistibly mischievous manner when he wanted something, and she really couldn't think of any more excuses to refuse.

Fortunately the excuse arrived then, in the pretty person of Victoria Sanchez. She stopped short when she saw Shelley on the bed and Miguel standing beside her, his fingers playing gently with her hair. 'Oh!' she exclaimed. She was wearing a tight black mini-dress, and her hair was a dark cloud around her beautiful face, the eyes made to look even larger by skilful dark blue make-up. 'Oh,' she said again. 'I'm sorry for barging in without ringing the bell.'

Shelley said quietly, 'That's all right, Victoria. I'm sure you have as much right to be here as anyone.' She repeated Miguel's words, which he had said to her only moments before. He looked down at her, and stroked back his hair. Shelley said, 'I'll take the jeep, shall I?'

CHAPTER NINE

FOR the next few days there was no sign of Miguel in the Monte Samana complex, and Shelley didn't go to the village, because he didn't get in touch to ask her to go. The new clinics weren't yet started, and she knew Miguel had not decided which day would be best. She said nothing about Miguel to Victoria for several days, and Victoria didn't broach the subject of finding both of them in Miguel's bedroom. She didn't seem annoyed with Shelley at all, but she too spoke only about work and about coming attractions at the complex, almost as though she was embarrassed to bring the subject up.

Finally Shelley felt she had to break the silence. In between patients she said to Victoria, 'There was nothing, that day, between Dr Rafaelo and me, you know.'

The other girl tossed her pretty dark hair back from her face and said casually, 'It is not my business.'

'But you did ask me once, and I said no. Remember?'

'I remember.' Victoria managed a smile, and looked up openly at Shelley from her desk. 'You said he was as important to you as a desk or a wardrobe!'

'Well, nothing's changed, I swear. The only difference between then and now is that I've decided to apply to extend my contract with him, and work in Santa Barbara more.'

'Yes, he told me.'

She might have known Victoria was in Miguel's confidence. She wished she hadn't mentioned it now. 'Oh, so there was no need for me to explain.'

'Not really.' Victoria was looking carefully into

125

Shelley's face for signs of prevarication. 'But surely you like him a little?'

'I like him quite a lot.' Shelley decided to be honest with this girl, who was so close to Miguel Rafaelo. 'But there's a great world of difference between liking and — anything deeper.'

Victoria said, 'Shelley, there's no need to tell me anything.'

'But there is. You have a prior claim on him. I don't want you to feel that I'm jealous, or anything like that.'

Victoria smiled again, and her long eyelashes flickered against her cheek. 'Shelley, Miguel Rafaelo is not a goldfield, where women can stake their claims! He makes up his own mind, and he is his own man. No one can make him do anything he doesn't want. So you see, Shelley, it isn't between you and me, or between any woman. It's between Miguel and the woman he chooses.'

Shelley nodded. 'I know that. I suppose I just didn't want you jumping to conclusions. I don't want you thinking I'm chasing him.'

'I know you aren't. Miguel does the chasing when it suits him. Anyone trying it the other way round is wasting her time.'

Shelley said, 'Well, I'm glad we sorted that out. And you do have a special place in his life, I'm sure of that.'

'Yes, I know I have.' The words weren't said triumphantly. Victoria just stated a simple fact, and it effectively ended the conversation.

Shelley and Rosie were lying by the pool one afternoon, Rosie didn't feel like swimming, complaining of indigestion, so Shelley stayed with her under the trees, totally idle and satisfied in the all-pervading heat. After a long time, a familiar voice woke them from their lazy reverie. 'I hope you agree that I can go for my regular swim again, Shelley?'

Shelley sat up with a jerk. 'Mrs Richards! How nice to see you looking so well.'

The old lady was dressed in a towelling wrap over a bathing suit. Behind her, also in a towelling wrap, walked Lina Freitas, carrying a bag containing some beach towels, sun-cream and Mrs Richards's parasol.

'Good afternoon, Señorita Shelley,' Lina smiled.

'Lina, you're swimming as well! I hope you're going to visit our Santa Barbara surgery regularly. Dr Rafaelo is seeing mothers and babies every week, you know.'

Mrs Richards said, 'You can count on me to look after her, Shelley. Lina helps me in the mornings, to dress and to arrange my clothes. Then she goes home——'

'In a taxi!' said the girl, impressed.

'In a taxi, and doesn't return until now. She'll stay with me while I swim, then we'll take a cup of tea together before she goes——'

'By taxi!'

'By taxi home again.'

Lina said, beaming, 'My English gets very good, Señorita Shelley, and Señorita Richards one day when she is stronger will come to Santa Barbara to meet my mother and my grandfather.'

'And your fiancé!' said Mrs Richards sharply. 'It's time he was a little more than a fiancé, in my opinion. Now come along. If it's all right with Shelley, we may take our swim.'

Shelley said, 'It's absolutely fine by Shelley—for both of you. Enjoy the water.'

Lina said to Shelley with a little grin, as her employer led the way down the grass towards the pool, 'Sometimes I think I will pretend to drown a little, to get Carlos to look at me. But I do not do it, because I do not wish to upset Señora Richards.'

'And because you're engaged to Pablo!'

'Oh, yes, that also!'

Rosie said, as they lay back, eyes narrowed in the sun, 'Are you going to tell me why you chose Lina? There must be village girls who aren't pregnant.'

'It's a long story, but basically I thought they'd get on together. And I was right.'

'But why?' asked Rosie. So Shelley told the story, in confidence. But when she was only halfway through, Rosie got up and said, 'I don't feel well, Shelley.' And she ran to the nearest ladies' room and emerged with bleary eyes, clutching at her stomach.

Shelley, already on her feet, carried her up to the medical centre with Carlos's help. She examined Rosie's abdomen, which tensed at her touch. 'This looks a lot like appendicitis,' she decided. 'I'm going to send you to the hospital, Rosie.'

Rosie nodded, and her voice was hoarse. 'Could you ask Francisco to find the woman who looked after the shop for me last time I was ill?'

'I'll do that. Lie back now, and I'll phone the hospital. Do you want me to take you in the jeep? I think you'd be better in an ambulance.'

'I don't care.' Rosie's face was distorted with pain now, and she writhed on the couch. Shelley wiped her forehead, and soothed her.

Just then Miguel came hurrying in. 'I was in Admin and they said Rosie was ill.' He took one look at the pale figure and said to Shelley, 'Is it appendix?'

'I'm almost sure.' Shelley looked up from her patient, surprised to find herself so pleased to see his reliable and comforting figure.

He examined Rosie carefully, and nodded. 'Go ahead, get the number. I'll take her in the Mercedes.'

'Shall I come?'

'I'm afraid you'll be needed here. I'll phone you as soon as there's any news. And you can visit tonight.' Miguel spoke on the crackling phone to the hospital surgeon, and soon patient and doctor were on their way, Rosie lying, with eyes tightly closed, on a stretcher. Shelley watched them go, recognising her own relief and pleasure at seeing Miguel. Don't get used to him! Don't rely on him! Her inner caution was warning her against this feeling, but was finding it hard to get through to her.

Rosie was operated on almost at once. The hospital phoned Miguel that evening, and he came to the villa to tell Shelley, who had been sitting by the telephone. 'It was a simple appendix. She is awake and happy that it's all over. But she is still too sleepy for visitors. She's asked you to go tomorrow night, Shelley — Saturday.'

'That's OK. I'll go with Francisco. I'll root out a change of nightclothes and some fruit. Poor old Rosie. Good job I was with her.'

Miguel was standing in the doorway, his handsome face in shadow. It was eleven o'clock at night, Shelley had already showered ready for bed, and now stood dressed only in her bathrobe, her feet bare. Miguel said, 'If you go visiting tomorrow night, you won't be able to go to Pepe's.'

Shelley hadn't realised the implications of visiting a hospital over eight miles away. 'I was assuming I'd be back before midnight. Anyway, it isn't compulsory to go to Pepe's.'

'But for you! I thought you were expecting to——'

'No, Miguel. I know Miguelito rang you, but he didn't ring me, so I don't feel I have to go. There's no date as far as I'm concerned.'

Miguel cleared his throat. 'Are you going to keep me here on the doorstep?'

She smiled at him, aware that he was angling for an invitation. 'Did you want to say anything else?'

'I wouldn't mind a cup of coffee.' His look was appealing, almost angelic.

'OK, come in, then.' He stepped over the threshold, brushing back his hair in that characteristic gesture, both modest and attractive. Shelley warned, 'But I am going to bed soon.' The more time she spent with

Miguel Rafaelo, the more she wanted to. It was strange how fascinating he was becoming to her, against her own wish that their relationship should remain strictly businesslike.

She led the way into the kitchen and spooned coffee into the jug. 'Sit down, Miguel. Coffee won't be long.'

'Poor Rosie — did you have no warning that this appendicitis was coming on?' he asked.

'No. She didn't want to swim this afternoon, but only said it was slight indigestion.'

'And you won't be lonely here in the villa alone? I could always arrange to stay to look after you.' His grin altered his steady, reliable image into a rather roguish one. Shelley smiled back, but she was well aware that he meant it, and that given half a chance he would stay the night. She handed him a mug of coffee and he thanked her. 'You're not having one?'

'I'm tired, and I don't want to be kept awake.'

'Are you trying to get rid of me?'

'No — what gave you that idea?'

'Oh, Shelley, Shelley, you're a beautiful woman, but you tease me too much.'

'I've no choice if I don't want to turn into number four!'

'Oh, don't go on about those women — they weren't a patch on you, you know. And I never encouraged any of them. And I didn't break any hearts — they all knew the score. I took them out as a favour to my employees.'

'And how do I know that isn't just what you're doing with me?'

'Because I'm here, Shelley, when I ought to be tucked up at home. Because I couldn't settle tonight until I knew you were all right.'

She smiled at him from the opposite stool. The atmosphere between them was so right, so good. She wouldn't mind this evening going on forever. 'You're very nice, Miguel. I do appreciate you — honestly.'

'But you're sending me home?'

He was her boss, her chief, yet tonight he was the one doing the pleading. She said gently, 'Oh, yes, I'm sending you home to Casa Madrid.'

He sipped the coffee. Then he stood up as though giving up. '*Bueno!* I'm on my way. Look after yourself, my dear, and sleep well.'

Shelley stood up too, to see him to the door. 'Goodnight, Miguel. Thanks for helping us.'

His kiss was gentle and without passion, but again it was long and sweet and searching. She didn't notice when he had taken his glasses off. Sensations running wild, Shelley put her arms round him, holding him close, unable to pretend that she didn't want him. In ready response, his embrace grew masterful, and they clung together as he kissed her face and neck repeatedly, each time catching her lips with more desire and more breathless pleasure. 'Miguel—oh, Miguel, please go now,' she heard herself murmuring, and he murmured his agreement, while still continuing his warm sweet exploration of her lips and tongue. She drew her head back, but he pressed it against him. His cheek was warm and smooth and very desirable, and she gave in, unable to push him away when having him close was so much more delightful.

It was Miguel who next drew back. 'I've been trying to go for the last half-hour,' he whispered, 'but you won't let go of my neck!'

'Oh, you cheat!' Shelley unclasped her hands and put them obediently at her sides. 'There!'

He smiled at her lazily, his eyes soft and beautiful without the glasses. Then he reached out and tousled her hair with gentle fingers. '*Buenas noches, querida.*' He closed the door behind him, and Shelley stood in the hall for a long time, one hand up to her untidy hair where Miguel had ruffled it.

* * *

Rosie was sitting propped against pillows, looking tired but relieved. 'I should have told you earlier about the pain, Shelley, but I thought you'd had enough ill people for one day,' she explained.

'Oh, you goose. Well, you'll be OK now. Back with us in a few days.'

'There are some things I need from the villa, Shelley.'

'More than this? No problem. Give me a list, I'll bring them next time.'

'But what about tonight?'

'What about tonight?'

'It's Saturday, and you haven't missed a Saturday at Pepe's since you arrived. You must go now or you'll miss your hero.'

'No, really—I don't really want to go anyway. I'll see him next week.' With all the activity surrounding her friend, Shelley had forgotten what day it was. Pepe's Bar day. And last Sunday Miguelito had rung Miguel to ask if he could meet her again. She had exactly six hours till midnight, six hours to make up her mind whether to go down to the beach bar, or give it a miss for the very first time. It seemed unthinkable to turn Miguelito down now, after that warm flush of pleasure just thinking about being with him, his strong body and arms, his soft mouth and deep beautiful voice.

But Rosie had come first, and real people mattered more than fantasies. Perhaps if she hurried she could get back to the complex in time for Miguelito's spot. If not, then—he would still be there next week.

Just as well—for Francisco got lost. It had been all right finding the hospital, but on the way back he took a wrong turn and ended up by the seaside. Asking the way towards Monte Samana, they found themselves back at the hospital. By the time he had found the way, it was after midnight, the clock had chimed ages ago, and Shelley could do nothing but walk up the hill to go home to bed. She paused outside the villa, and looked round at the dark hills against the starry sky. She looked out to the shore and thought about her dashing singer. It had been special, being with him last week, being the centre of his attention. But this was the real world, and young women like Shelley just didn't fit in with men like Miguelito. It was just a memory now, one that would stay with her forever. No matter who she met in the future, that walk in the lemon-scented night with him would be one part of her she would never share with anyone.

'Shelley?' She froze. Someone was walking up the hill, and his whisper echoed in the cypresses. '*Shelley, eres tu?*'

Her voice was a whisper. 'Miguelito?'

'*Sí. Por que, Shelley?*'

'My friend is sick—in hospital.' She turned as he reached her, hardly out of breath after his steep climb. 'It was too late to come, we got lost in the town.'

She could just see by the light of the wrought-iron lamps that he was wearing a shirt with frilled sleeves, and that his hair fell about his face. He stood close to her, and she felt the heat from his body. 'You would have come if you could?' he asked.

'I don't know.

'Why?'

She said, looking down, although it was too dark for him to see her blushing, 'That first time—I wanted to meet you, Miguelito, very much. But I don't think—it should go on. That night was a special memory for me. But there's no future in a relationship, and you have your secrecy to guard.'

In his gentle Spanish he said softly, 'I don't see it that way. I do not ask for sex right away. Why not a relationship? I am only a man like any other, and you are a very pretty girl. Come down with me and dance at the Casablanca Club. You don't know how many girls have begged me to come to the Casablanca Club, and you are the only one I have asked.'

Shelley's senses turned violent somersaults, and she wasn't responsible for her words as they tumbled out. 'I — my duty is to my — my job and my boss. There are projects we're working on in Santa Barbara that — — '

'Ha! That is it! I, Miguelito, cannot compete with your ordinary boss. You know, Shelley, I suspected there was something between you and Rafaelo the first time I talked to him. He was very protective about you. And now you confirm it.'

'Me and Miguel? What made you think that? I was only telling you that I'm going to be busy, and wouldn't make a good companion for you.'

He took her shoulders gently in his hands. 'Shelley, I am not an amateur in matters of love. I recognised at once that your chief is very important to your happiness. You may not know it, but by your emotion, I know.'

She looked up at the outline of him, the wild hair and the shadowed eyes. 'I'm crazy, and when I come to my senses I'll know that I'm crazy to admit it to anyone. But yes, Miguel Rafaelo matters to me, as a doctor, you understand — a good doctor, and as a friend.'

'I knew it. He is number one in your life now. Don't argue with me — I know what I see. One day we will meet again, Shelley. I go now.'

'*Pero* — —'

'*Adiós, mi querida.*' And the crunching of the gravel faded. Shelley went indoors, hardly realising what she had done. Miguelito the magnificent was hers for the taking, and she had sent him away, frills and all.

On Monday morning Shelley was early down at the medical centre. '*Hola*, Victoria,' she smiled.

'*Hola*. You couldn't sleep?'

'It's not the same without Rosie.'

Victoria said, 'I know. Miguel told me that Rosie is doing well, and might come home on Wednesday.'

Somehow Shelley's happy mood wilted, as she thought of Miguel relaying the news to his little friend in their Casa Madrid love nest. But Shelley put a brave face on the week. 'Yes, I might have known they wouldn't want Rosie there for too long. She talks too much.'

Someone pushed open the door, and Victoria greeted the newcomer with a torrent of Spanish. It was Lina Freitas. She said, 'I go to my mistress, but *señoritas*, first I invite you both to my wedding.' And when the congratulations and kisses had died down, she went on, 'Señorita Shelley, without you I could not dream of finding such a wonderful mistress. She buy for Pablo and me a house with furniture, and she consent to be godmother to our child.'

'God be praised,' said Victoria, kissing her again. 'God bless you, Lina, and make your marriage happy.'

'I owe my mistress everything, and I am very sad because she is old and will not live to see my child growing up.'

Shelley said, 'She will be around for a while, Lina, especially if you look after her, and treat her like your own *abuela*.'

'She is my *abuelita* already in my heart, Señorita Shelley—so kindly, and so understanding to me and my family. Her Spanish is very good, but she speaks to me in English to help me learn it.'

Shelley asked, 'She has met your family yet?'

'Not yet, but she promises to meet them at my wedding.'

As the girl ran off, her pretty face glowing with happiness, Victoria said, 'Mrs Richards has told me her story, Shelley. Do you really think the boy she loved all those years ago was really Felipe Freitas?'

Shelley nodded. 'The name fits, the time fits, and

the place fits. What more proof do you want? Is there another Felipe Freitas in this area?'

Victoria agreed. 'You're right—but if Mrs Richards has guessed the truth, what will it do to Felipe? He is a simple man, and old. The shock might be too great for him.'

Shelley said, 'Put yourself in his position, Victoria.'

'How could I? I've never been in love!'

Her words cut Shelley off, and for a moment she sat wondering if Miguel knew his beautiful Victoria didn't love him. He mattered to Shelley very much—as a doctor and as a person, and she couldn't bear to think of him losing that precious heart to this young girl, who regarded him just as someone to pay her bills.

Victoria's words cut into her thoughts. 'Go on, Shelley—what will old Freitas do when he meets his Constanza?'

Shelley said shortly, 'He'll be happy, Victoria. You don't need to go to school to know that.'

'But what will happen?'

Shelley looked at the date she had scribbled on to the surgery diary. 'We'll soon know. The wedding is next week.'

Francisco drove them to see Rosie next day. She was lively, and longing to be home. 'Apart from having to walk bent over, I'm fine,' she told them. 'The sooner I'm in that pool again, the happier I'll be.'

'And me,' said Francisco. 'I've been running the shop for you, Rosita.'

Rosie gave him an affectionate kiss, and Shelley decided that she needed to go for a walk around the hospital, to leave the two together for a while. She had never thought Rosie's friendship with Francisco was the long-standing sort, but it looked as though this sudden illness had drawn them together. Shelley allowed her imagination to run wild, picturing Rosie and Francisco working permanently at Monte Samana, and Shelley living in Santa Barbara. Miguel would control affairs from the Casa Madrid. Sometimes they would get together, swim at the cove, eat the Spanish way, siesta in the heat of the day, and life would be sweet and lazy and dripping with olives, vines and honey.

On the way back Francisco asked Shelley about Miguel. 'To me he is the boss, Shelley, the big man who gives the orders. Monte Samana is his, I know that now, and he deserves his profits, because he has made a holiday place that sits on the side of the hill as though it were set there by the Spaniards themselves, the Andalusians and the descendants of the Moors.'

She agreed with Francisco. 'He was a man with a dream. Like any good dream, it involved the welfare of all the people, not just himself.'

'The locals are praying that he wants to stay in Santa Barbara forever. If he put the running of this complex in other hands, it could never be the same.'

'I don't think he wants to leave, Francisco—not after starting all the clinics and welfare services for the people of the village.'

'I wondered if perhaps he was training you to take over from him,' he said. 'He has spent a lot of time showing you how his welfare works. A man like that gets restless. He might want to move on and repeat his success somewhere else.'

'I hadn't thought of that. But it does sound like a possibility.' Shelley was very thoughtful for the rest of the journey. Her vision of a happy life in Santa Barbara wouldn't be quite so blissful if Miguel were not resident in Casa Madrid.

When she met Miguel Rafaelo at the medical centre later in the week, she didn't have the nerve to ask him straight out. He was in a cheerful mood, in spite of his severe look, his scraped-back hair, conservative clothes and businesslike glasses. She said, 'I'm sure you've been invited to the wedding next week.'

'Yes. The family said if I couldn't come they would change the date.'

'Mrs Richards succeeded in getting the couple together.'

'Mrs Richards, God bless her, put down good money for them. They have a good start now. Lina was reluctant to leave a happy secure home, but now she will have a cottage of her own, with hot water and an indoor toilet and cooker, and grazing space for a couple of goats and many chickens. She told me she was looking forward to controlling her own home and her own destiny.'

'And controlling Pablo,' said Shelley, smiling. 'It takes a tough woman to control a Spanish man.'

'Really? And on what authority do you base this observation?'

Shelley laughed, and refused to be drawn. 'Back to work! When do I start going down to do the over-sixties' clinic?'

'We'll leave it until after the wedding. The entire population will be celebrating, and no one will give a *centavo* for their health until the *vino* runs dry.'

Shelley smiled. 'I want to be there when Lina introduces Mrs Richards to old Freitas.'

'You are convinced he was her childhood sweetheart?'

'Almost. If not, it doesn't matter. They're nice old people, and I think it would be good for Mrs Richards to come down to the village more, and be part of Santa Barbara.'

Miguel was sitting at his desk, and he reached over and pulled Shelley towards him, so that he could put his arm round her waist. 'To hear you speak about Santa Barbara, one would think you were a resident yourself.'

'I am. It's as much my home as yours, Miguel. You have a year or two's advantage on me, but I'll still be here when you're off looking for fresh fields to conquer.'

'Off? Me? Shelley, you have the wrong man. What makes you think I want any other fields than those right here in my home village?'

She smiled at him and gently disentangled his arm. 'You don't know how glad I am to hear you say that.'

'Why?'

'Because the village deserves the best, and they're getting it. Now that we're in the EC, there's no reason why our olives and our melons and our grapes can't bring real prosperity.'

'And I thought you were glad because we could spend some time together.'

'I can't think why you thought that.'

'Shelley?' His hand had caught hers again and held it very tightly. 'Will you come to Pepe's with me on Saturday?'

'I don't think I want to go there.'

'Why not? It's time you learnt to flamenco.'

She smiled at him, feeling the natural friendship and the closeness between them. 'Somehow I don't think that's for me, Miguel. Anyway, why don't you take Victoria?'

'Why her? She's a child.'

Shelley looked at him with surprise. 'You don't mean that. Have you looked at her lately?'

He shrugged. 'She's a pretty child. So what's new? I want you to come to Pepe's with me.'

Shelley said gently, 'I think I've outgrown Pepe's. Why don't you come to the villa, and I'll cook you a meal and we can listen to the folk singer by the pool?'

Miguel looked troubled. 'That's something I'd like very much, and it's also special because it's the first time you've invited me home. But I'm in a meeting until quite late—that's why I suggested Pepe's, because we don't have to be there till midnight. Please come, Shelley. I'll let you cook on Sunday.'

She was surprised at his insistence. 'And I thought you rather looked down on Miguelito and his fake charm?'

'I enjoy his playing. He's good.'

'Then you go. There are lots of girls to dance with.'

He pursed his lips and looked at her with a frown. 'If you change your mind, I'll pick you up at eight. You only have to phone me.' And he scraped his hair back, still frowning.

Shelley was intrigued by this first clash of wills between them. She said, 'I mean it when I say something, Miguel.'

'OK, OK, then I'll have to go alone. And I thought you were my friend, Shelley.'

'Your friend, yes — your poodle, no.'

He stood up and put his arm round her waist, giving it a quick squeeze. 'Never mind. Another time, eh?' And he strode out. In a moment she heard the engine of the Mercedes, and she heard it zoom down the hill with a squeal of tyres. If she didn't know him better, she would have said he was cross with her.

CHAPTER TEN

ROSIE and Francisco were spending Saturday night at home. 'I'm cooking, Shelley,' Francisco told her. 'You don't know what you're missing.'

'No offence, Francisco, but two's company. I'll go down to the pool and have a barbecue there. Back about midnight, I'd say.'

'You're not going to Pepe's?'

'What is this? Can't I stay away from Pepe's for once?'

'Pity to break the record,' said Rosie, with a smile.

'Just the right time to break the record. I'm about to sign a new contract that makes me virtually a Santa Barbara resident, and we locals don't mix with you tourists!'

Rosie joked, 'Hey, less of the tourists! I've lived here longer than you. But seriously, I'm very happy that you're staying. The only problem is—Francisco and I are buying this villa from Mum and Dad. We're going to live here for good, Shelley. When we fix a date, we'd like you to be bridesmaid.'

Shelley looked at the happy faces of her companions, and knew they wanted to be alone, however sweet they were being. 'What marvellous news. I'm thrilled to bits. And I know what you're saying, Rosie—I'm going to have to find new digs. No problem—I'd love to live in Santa Barbara.' She laughed. 'The only thing will be getting used to no air-conditioning, but I think I can live with that. I'll start looking out for somewhere to live next time I go down. I quite fancy a cottage near the town square—handy for work.'

Francisco said, 'You have settled down in Spain

much faster than Rosie. She needed four years before she knew she wanted to live here. What made it so easy for you to make your mind up?'

Shelley considered for a moment. 'Who can say? I just feel at home here.'

'I blame Miguelito!' Rosie teased.

'Nothing to do with him.' But Shelley admitted that she had fallen in love with his music, which made it easier to like everything else Spanish. 'Having a decent boss helped.' She walked through the open window to the balcony. 'But just look at that view — and feel the loving warmth all around! How could anyone seriously want to go back to wind and rain and the grey walls and streets of north Britain forever? I'll go back to visit, naturally, out of affection for the place. But for me, home is here.'

Rosie walked out to join her, her limp almost gone. 'What was that earlier remark about your boss?'

'Nothing much — only that Miguel is such a nice person. He thinks the same way as I do about our work. He's done so much good around here — I know it's going to be inspiring working for him.'

'Shelley, I do hope you aren't getting too fond of him.'

'Nothing of the sort. Admiration has nothing at all to do with — falling in love, that sort of thing. I'm immune to him, I assure you.'

Rosie looked hard at her, but Shelley kept her chin up, and her gaze direct. Rosie said, 'Stay and eat with us, Shelley.'

'No — but thank you.'

Francisco said, 'I'm really pleased you're going to be around, Shelley. Life is going to be like one long happy holiday.'

'I hope so. And thanks for asking me to be bridesmaid. Another wedding to look forward to after Lina and Pablo. I love weddings.' Shelley left the balcony and came in. 'But now I must go. I've kept you from your dinner long enough.'

She walked down the hill, leaving the jeep parked by the villa. If she had taken the jeep, she knew she would have been tempted to drive it to the beach and look in at Pepe's. Tonight she had resolved to make the break with the tourist side of herself. Let dear old Miguelito charm a new generation of English roses — Shelley had outgrown him, although she would always keep a special place in her inner being for that lovely evening when she and only she had had his sweet and undivided attention... No one could ever take that away from her, and she would always think of him with special affection.

The girl singer was in good voice by the pool, singing some sentimental Spanish favourites, with that wistful lilt that gave them their distinctive charm. She waved to Shelley, and began to sing a song made famous by Miguelito, giving her a private lift of the eyebrows. Even Carmen knew that Shelley was the girl who loved Miguelito, and Shelley smiled and waved back, content for the fiction to be carried on. It was innocent fun.

The barbecue captain was effusive. 'You eat with us tonight, Señorita Shelley! You make me very happy. Tonight I find you the special number one steak, and the best wine.'

'Why make a fuss, Antonio?'

'It is sad to see such a beautiful woman eating alone.'

'Oh, Antonio, that's the way I like it!'

Another voice intruded into the conversation. Miguel Rafaelo said, 'Can you find me a good steak too, Antonio?'

'Only the very best for you, *señor*.' Antonio was positively bouncing with the honour of serving the big man himself.

'You don't mind if I sit here, Shelley?'

'No, of course not.' She was always glad to see

Miguel, and he was clearly not annoyed about her refusal to go to Pepe's. 'Do you remember bringing me here when I was very new to Monte Samana?'

'How could I forget? You lit up the night with your beauty.'

'Oh, sure.' Shelley gave him a smile that deflated his compliment without being ungracious. 'What brings you to Samana tonight? I thought you had a meeting?'

'A secret mission.' He whispered the words in her ear. 'Don't ask — it's classified.'

Antonio brought them wine and olives. The smell of the barbecue was at its most tempting, and the smoke from it writhed upwards towards the villa where Rosie and Francisco were. Shelley told Miguel about their engagement. 'So I'm looking for somewhere to live. I know there are apartments here on the complex, Miguel, but I think it would be nice to live in Santa Barbara.'

'I agree completely,' he said. 'You belong in Santa Barbara, and I'm sure if you let the villagers know, they will find you a house quite quickly. When do you want to move out?'

'No pressure, but now that I know about Francisco it makes sense to leave them as soon as I find something suitable.'

'Trust me — I'll be your agent.'

Shelley laughed. 'Miguel, I have to trust you! Who else? My future is in your hands.'

'You do feel happy about making the commitment to Santa Barbara? It is your own choice, not affected by what I want?'

'Of course it is. I'm a free spirit, thanks to you, Miguel. And yes, I know I'm beautiful, if you say so, but what matters more to me is that I'm a damn good nurse and I have something to give to these people.'

'A free spirit? And beautiful. Shelley, what more can you want out of life? Love maybe? A beautiful woman shouldn't be alone!'

'Don't try to indoctrinate me, Miguel. I'm happy with my life.'

The steaks arrived, with a huge mixed salad and olive oil dressing. Between mouthfuls Shelley explained to Miguel how her happiness had materialised. 'This time last year I was cold and very miserable. You were quite right about Ken Noakes—my experience with him had temporarily made me lose faith in men, and in myself. The cold of the weather was reflected by the coldness of my own personality. I admit it freely, and I admit that you were the first to make the diagnosis.'

Miguel placed his knife and fork on the empty plate and turned to her. 'What else will you admit to, Shelley? That you would like to spend Saturday night with me?' He took her hand in his and murmured, 'Otherwise I'll be very lonely.'

'Me too,' she said, thinking of the happy couple up in the villa. Rosie and Francisco were together, and as she looked around she realised she was surrounded by couples. She looked him in the eye and admitted, 'If you have nothing better to do, I'd like to be with you, Miguel.'

He took her hand in his. 'You're beginning to own that you have feelings for me. That is good.'

'Only tonight, because I'm a little lonely. I'm not likely to fall for you, you know. I know your past reputation.' She laughed at his outraged expression. 'It's fun having a boss like you, though, and I know I'll enjoy working for you in Santa Barbara.'

'That prim little British heart is safe from me, is it, Shelley?'

'You know very well that I decided that months ago—and nothing's changed.'

Miguel drained his glass. 'Come, Shelley—the night is young, and I feel adventurous.'

'I hope you have your pager with you!'

'Thank you for bringing my feet down to the ground. Yes, I have the mobile phone in the car. Shall we go?'

There was no getting away from the fact that sometimes being with Miguel made Shelley feel happier than she had ever been in her life. He had the ability, when he was in that teasing mood, to make her forget all the worrying unhappy things in life, and just be gloriously glad to be alive. She felt bubbly with fun, and had to try hard not to let it show too much.

He drove down to the beach, but did not park near Pepe's. She was thankful for that, because she didn't want to see Miguelito tonight. He was part of her past now, and the future was a little more serious and a lot more dedicated. She looked at her handsome companion, who stuck to his sleeked-back hairstyle even when relaxed. He turned and caught her looking at him as they strolled idly along by the whispering dark Mediterranean, and impulsively he stopped and pulled her into his arms for a quick hard hug. She laid her cheek contentedly against his chest, and hugged him back. There was just a tiny blot on her happiness, and that was the knowledge that one day this man would want to settle down, and when he did she felt sure he would choose the companion of his last four years, the pretty Victoria.

As they walked on, he started to talk about her future contract, and as he did so he put his arm about her shoulders and held her close. Shelley reflected that they must look less like a doctor and a nurse discussing their clinic rota, and a lot more like a couple in love murmuring sweet nothings. 'So is a ten-year agreement too much to ask?' he was saying.

'I'm quite agreeable to that, as long as the wording is such that if we find each other horrendously incompatible after each year there's a let-out clause.'

'You are so flattering!' he teased. 'We've managed very well so far.'

'That's why I'm cautious. Maybe it's gone very well

because neither of us is—well, committed to anyone else. If one of us marries—well, the demands of a household on top of a medical practice might prove too much of a strain.'

'That might be true of you, Shelley, dear, but remember, I run a successful business as well as a medical practice, so having a wife as well shouldn't make much difference.'

'You're joking! You wouldn't be able to walk along the Malecon with me like this, for a start!'

'And would you miss this?' he whispered in her ear, his breath tickling her.

'Naturally, for a while.'

'So you would be a tiny bit jealous?'

'Nonsense. Just—different, because you'd be tied up elsewhere, and I would have to look for other friends. But it won't matter—I'm sure I can soon find friends.'

'Not as good as me, though, eh, Shelley?' She hadn't even noticed where they were, but now he was guiding her up some stone steps, and she realised by the background music that they were heading for Pepe's. 'I have to see someone for a minute. Wait for me inside.'

'All right. What time is it?'

'Nearly midnight. Won't be long.' And they went in together, the beat of the music throbbing through the night sky.

His arm was still round her, as Pepe called, '*Hola, muchachos*!' from behind the bar.

'*Hola, Pepe.*' Miguel led Shelley behind the bar and behind the beaded curtain into the private section of Pepe's.

She said, 'You're meeting Miguelito!' accusingly.

'You don't mind, do you? I won't take a minute.' And he pushed open a small wooden door. Inside the room was a table and a chair facing a mirror. There was a guitar on the table, and a frilled black silk shirt hanging up behind the door. Miguelito's room, for sure. Miguel slipped off his casual shoes and began to pull on the black cuban-heeled boots he picked up from the floor. Pepe tapped on the door and came in with two glasses of what looked like rum and cola. '*Ah, gracias, Pepe,*' said Miguel. '*Uno para Shelley? Gracias.*'

'Miguel——?' Shelley was beginning to see something that she didn't like at all.

'*Sí, mi amor?*' He had taken his glasses off now and pulled his T-shirt up over his head, revealing that manly torso of perfect proportions, over which he deftly fastened the frilled silk shirt, and tucked it into his jeans. His hair curled around his face, and he went to a small basin and swilled water from the tap, rubbing his face and head briskly with a towel. The transformation was almost complete. When he picked up the guitar, slung it round his neck, and started to tune the strings, there was no more doubt.

'You *are* Miguelito.'

'*Sí, mi amor*. And you are the only person apart from Pepe who knows my secret. Now do you see how much you mean to me?'

She felt herself blushing scarlet. 'I see how much of a fool you've made of me!'

Miguel finished tuning the guitar and turned to look at her, obviously perturbed at the sudden anger in her voice. 'I thought——'

'I know what you thought. You clearly don't know anything about women's pride. Don't you see——?' But the church bell was chiming outside, and the dance-floor in the little café was falling silent.

Miguel put his finger on her lips and whispered, 'Please wait for me. I will only sing one song.'

'Don't hurry on my account! Sing a million for all I care!'

Miguel seemed torn. 'Shelley——' But the last stroke had sounded, its echo drifting away into the night, and with a frown of anxiety, he pulled himself away from her and disappeared through the door. Shelley heard the shouts and whistles as their favourite glamour-boy appeared to his fans. With a frustrated sob of despair and shame, she followed him out. Through the beaded curtain she could see the devoted gaze of the women in the front row. No one even noticed her as she slipped out into the dance-floor, and made her way out down the rickety steps. It was a warm and friendly night, and the sea swished and whispered on the sand. But all Shelley felt was a wild desire to get away. She ran, ran from the memory of her own besottedness with this man, painfully aware what a fool she had made of herself before him, how she had opened her heart to him. She ran, with his voice, that deep and beautiful voice she had loved so much, following her along the beach, as though it mocked her.

She ran almost all the way through the town. Breathless, she slowed to a walk through the lemon groves near the complex, and by the time she reached Monte Samana she had slowed to a snail's pace. Her tears had been angry tears at first, but now they were sad and bitter. How foolishly happy she had been earlier that evening, and how ridiculous she felt at this moment, all her dreams crushed and shattered around her slowly dragging feet.

She walked up to the villa. It was in darkness, and she let herself in and stepped out of her clothes, throwing herself into bed, too miserable now for tears. She slept almost at once, a great weariness overwhelming her, but even in her sleep she knew she was unhappy.

When she woke, the misery was still there. How could she face Rosie and Francisco? But then she reminded herself that Miguel had entrusted her with his secret, and there was no way she could even explain her unhappiness to anyone. She tried to think of something to say. 'We had an argument.' That certainly didn't sound serious enough to account for her great grief. Better to say nothing, and try to pretend she was just tired.

Fortunately Rosie and Francisco went out after breakfasting, and, thinking Shelley was still asleep, they didn't knock on her door. At least she had the villa to herself to be miserable in. She made some coffee, and went out on the balcony in her cotton housecoat, where she could see the sun rising from behind the dark hills, and the slopes slowly become bathed with light. She felt as though she was seeing them from under a great weight. But in the sweet and gentle light of day, she began to face herself, to think back over the conversation she had with 'Miguelito', and to try and work out just how besotted she had sounded to him.

It wasn't fair. No matter which way she looked at it, he had no right to allow her to make a fool of herself. They had discussed him—what had she said about Miguel to 'Miguelito'? And he actually expected her to be pleased to be let into his secret! In her mind she went over the transformation. The glasses came off, and the hair was allowed to fall freely in its natural waves around his face. The shirt with full sleeves, the boots and the guitar, slowly turning her nice conservatively dressed Dr Rafaelo into the glamorous and dashing young singer, speaking only in Spanish, every girl's heart-throb.

No wonder he had never allowed the spotlight to catch him full face. Once his identity was known, he would have to give up the singing. And it had become such a popular feature of Samana life. He must have started as a joke, to indulge his love of singing and of local folk music. No doubt he had not expected to become so popular and idolised. Yes, and Shelley Cameron had been fool enough to do some of that idolising! Well, what a way to grow up. What a miserable and hurtful way to come to terms with herself.

She looked at the cold cup of coffee on the table, and left it there while she went in to shower and put on some clothes, shorts and a T-shirt and tennis shoes. It was such a lovely day, and there was so much to do on the complex, but Shelley couldn't summon the enthusiasm to leave the villa. She went out into the small back garden, and sat on the tiled patio in a canvas chair, staring at nothing.

'I never meant to hurt you, Shelley.'

She looked up sullenly. Miguel stood before her, his face grave. Automatically his hand went up to scrape his hair back over his ears. She said, 'How did you get in?'

'I just walked round the house.'

He was wearing jeans and a dark blue polo-shirt. She said bitterly, 'Where's your fancy shirt today, Miguel?'

'That's all over. I've told Pepe to put a notice up that Miguelito has gone for a holiday abroad.'

Shelley said dully, 'There was no reason to stop doing it. It was well liked among the Samana people.'

'My heart has gone out of it.'

'You didn't honestly expect me to stay, did you?'

For a moment there was a flash of anger. 'I can't see why a spot of honesty has upset you so much. At least be flattered that I chose you to tell the truth to.'

She said quietly, with no tone in her voice, 'To make an idiot out of, you mean. I don't really want to talk to you any more. Please go away.'

'No, I won't. Not until you have seen reason.'

'You might own this place, Miguel, and you might have the right to stand where you like on it, but you'll never make me pleased to see you ever again. Is that clear?'

'It's clear—and it's stupid.'

'If the big man says it's stupid, then of course it must

be. I'm only the nurse. What Miguel says goes around here, I dare say. I'd still like to be left to my own company.'

'Now look here, Shelley, you can't pretend that you don't care about me, because I happen to know you do.'

'I was such a little silly, wasn't I, pouring out my precious little thoughts and fears to nice big Miguelito!' She stood up suddenly, so that she could stamp the floor, annoyed because tennis shoes couldn't make a big enough noise to suit her fury. 'You had no right, no right at all, to cheat me like that, to con me into thinking I could trust you. Well, I tell you this for nothing, and this is the truth. I never want to talk to you again about anything else but work.'

'That's impossible, and you know it is. Shelley, you mean so much to me—come down to the pool, and let's talk things over quietly. After all, no harm is done. Nobody knows anything about this except you and me, and we are friends, aren't we, Shelley? We'll always be friends, I know it.' She didn't answer, and his tone became softer and more wheedling. There was no disguising that he had a beautiful deep voice, thrillingly sensual when he chose to be. But it only reminded Shelley of Miguelito, and she turned away, her anger rising again. 'In fact, what you said was very beautiful and sweet. It did you credit. It only revealed what a warm, decent nature you have.' He paused. 'It made me love you more, Shelley.'

His words hung in the air between them, in that cypress-scented garden. The sparrows twittered and fluttered under the eaves, and the sound of children's laughter floated up from the pool down the hill. But Shelley was unable to get rid of the sense of shame, of being exposed and cheated. She didn't turn, didn't speak. The silence dragged on. She could even hear the little lizards darting on scratchy little claws among the bougainvillaea on the low ornamental wall.

The repetitive purr of the telephone broke into the fragile atmosphere, and Shelley walked past Miguel without looking at him to go into the villa. She picked it up. '*Hola?*'

'Nurse Shelley? Please come quickly. A child has been brought in after choking on a plum stone.'

'Unconscious?'

'Just coming round.'

'I'm on my way.'

Miguel had followed her into the room. 'We'll take my car. It's at the gate. It will be quicker.'

'Right.' She was calm now. Her training, and her experience, had taught her to put the patient first, whatever her own feelings might be. Miguel Rafaelo was now only a colleague in an emergency. 'You heard the problem?' she asked. They were in the Mercedes now, and Miguel was already putting his foot down, skidding a little on the gravel of the road as he took the bends. 'A child choked on a fruit stone.'

'Unconscious, you said.'

'Just coming round.'

Miguel said, 'Then the emergency is over, wouldn't you say?'

'She's probably swallowed the stone. The airways are clear, but it might lodge in the oesophagus.'

'Would you send her for X-ray?'

Shelley said shortly, 'Depends on her condition. Let's take a look first, shall we?'

The little girl was about four, a pretty child with curly fair hair and chubby cheeks. She was sitting on her mother's knee, and the receptionist was standing by the desk, with a form already filled with her name and address. 'This is Samantha, Dr Rafaelo. She was blue when they carried her in, but it looks as though the stone has gone down the right way.'

The mother looked worried. 'But surely you have to operate to get it out?'

Miguel smiled reassuringly. 'The human body has a

very efficient way of getting rid of useless waste, *señora*. Shall I just check Samantha's throat?' He examined the girl, felt the chest and abdomen, then made her drink a large glass of water. 'I think the stone will appear after about twenty-four hours, *señora*. Let her have plenty to drink, and call me or Nurse Cameron at once if you're worried.'

The mother and child went out happily, and the receptionist went back to the admin building. Miguel took the card and wrote on it what had been done for Samantha. Shelley waited, unsure whether to stay on here. Miguel looked up. 'Well, I think we ought to go to Santa Barbara. Are you ready?'

'I think it would be better if you go on alone today.'

'I never had you down as a quitter.'

'I'm not. But is there anyone special to see? I don't want to come there and find I have nothing to do.'

'There is a patient you sent to me for tests — the man with anorexia, you remember? He has agreed to come and see me this morning, if you're interested.'

'Well, yes, I am. The husband of Inés Lopez. Was anything abnormal found in the alimentary canal?'

'Come along and see.'

'If I won't be in your way.' They were distantly polite to each other now, keeping the conversation strictly about work.

'Not at all. As you saw the man first, I think you would be interested to interview him now, and see if his attitude to himself has altered.'

She sat stiffly in the Mercedes, unwilling to continue the conversation. The familiar ride past the saluting gateman, past the lemon groves and the sharp roundabout to the little dirt road that was Santa Barbara's main street, was tinged with an overwhelming gloom in spite of its beauty. Paradise was well and truly lost. In its place only a sense of duty and a wish to be of help to the people she had come to love kept Shelley from despair.

She watched the top of Miguel's dark head as he examined the villager, and felt a wave of misery threaten to engulf her. To think this man she had thought so highly of could stoop to cheat and mislead her. With an enormous sense of loss, she looked at him, at his gentle eyes, behind the glasses, the sensitive fingers and that deep reassuring voice.

Miguel looked up at her suddenly, caught her staring, and hesitated in what he was saying, as though he understood what was going on in her mind. 'Er — as I was saying, Shelley, there is nothing physically wrong with Señor Lopez. His wife has told him to pull himself together. Do you think he will believe us if we tell him that?'

Shelley sat down beside the patient and smiled at him, the cheerfulness coming from somewhere behind her deep despair. 'I know there's nothing wrong with you, Señor Lopez, except a certainty that because your brother and your father suffered from cancer you will automatically get it. Nothing's further from the truth. You're a fit man, and you're frightening your wife and making yourself unhappy by letting your mind dwell on this. But to be honest, I can't think what we can do to stop you. You've convinced yourself you're ill, and only you can come to realise that you're as well as Dr Rafaelo or me.'

Miguel said quietly, 'I have an idea. You are a carpenter, yes?'

'Yes, *señor*, I work from home.'

'And you live here, in the main street?'

'Yes, *señor*.'

'Then you are just the man I need,' said Miguel. 'I want an archway built in my garden in time for the wedding of Lina and Pablo next Saturday. The dancing will be held there in the evening. It is to be finished by Friday, so that the girls can decorate it with flowers. I know exactly how I want it to look, Señor Lopez, but I don't know exactly how to do it. Can you help me?

The difficulty is how to make places for the flowers so that they won't fall out.'

The man's face brightened and he lost his hangdog expression as he spoke. 'That is easy—make the arch in the shape of a bent tree trunk, and make holes in the branches big enough to place pots of water, to make the flowers stay fresh for longer.'

'Won't that show?'

'Oh, no, *señor*—we bring plenty of moss from the hills and cover all the pots so that they appear to be part of the tree. May I come up and see the place you want it?'

Shelley watched them go, her heart full of admiration for his humanity and his talent—and bitterness because he had made such a fool of her.

CHAPTER ELEVEN

'SHELLEY CAMERON, how can you say such a thing! I've never heard such nonsense!' Rosie was in a high old state with her best friend. 'You can't stay away from the wedding! You of all people. After all you've done for that family. And I know very well how much you love them all—especially the old rogue Abuelo Freitas. They'd be so disappointed—and hurt, I'd say. It would be the height of bad manners, and I know you aren't that sort of person. Anyway, what on earth brought this on? You've been looking forward to this wedding for days now. It doesn't make any sort of sense to back out now.'

In spite of her black depression, Shelley had to smile. 'Well, thank goodness you had to stop for breath. You really know how to make a girl feel good!'

'Well, it is totally ridiculous and you know it.'

Shelley sighed deeply. 'I suppose I do. I suppose I wouldn't really stay away. But I don't feel very festive. Maybe I've been working too hard.'

'All the more reason to look forward to a happy day off.'

Shelley nodded. 'I'll be there.'

'Right—then back to my original question—what are we going to wear?'

'Something bright and pretty, I guess.' Shelley was very offhand.

'That's not like you, Shelley! As long as I've known you, you always give the subject of clothes the deep respect it deserves! You'll be telling me next that you don't really care if the earrings go with the dress!'

'Something like that. Look, Rosie, it's Lina's day. Does it matter what the guests wear?'

'Yes, it jolly well does, because it's a compliment to the bride to dress up on her special day.'

'All right, Rosie, let's look through the wardrobes.'

'I was thinking more along the lines of—let's go to the boutique.'

Shelley laughed, teased for a moment out of her blues. 'All right, I'll come with you to the boutique. Their stuff is overpriced, but I suppose a wedding is a wedding.'

In the boutique near the admin bulding the first person they saw was Mrs Richards. 'Hello, Shelley and Rosie—how nice to see you. I really need some advice about what to wear for the wedding.'

'Then we're at your service.' Rosie was already rifling along the rows of dresses.

Shelley knew that there was more to Constance Richards's desire to look good. It wasn't only the bride, but the bride's family she was to meet for the first time. And of that family, old Abuelo himself. Shelley said, making sure nobody could hear them, 'Do you think Abuelo is your Felipe?'

The pale old eyes were bright with hope. 'I'm almost sure. Lina has talked of his wartime experiences, and yes, he was reported missing. Tell me, Shelley, is he still good-looking?'

'He is.' For a man of his years, Abuelo was distinguished. 'I must say the old trousers he wears let him down a little—but at the wedding he'll wear his best suit. And thank goodness he's thrown away that smelly pipe.'

'Ragged trousers...dirty old pipe? It doesn't conjure up any very glamorous pictures,' smiled the old lady.

'I hope you won't be disappointed,' said Shelley. 'After all, it was all my doing, getting you to meet the family.'

'I'll be glad to get to know them all, even if he isn't

the man I once knew. They do sound like good people. I hope they like me.'

'No problem in that department. Now, Mrs Richards, have you thought of trying something in blue, to match your eyes?'

It was a long morning, but after many hours and a lot of giggling and parading, the three of them had chosen dresses. Rosie knew her cuddly frame looked best in plain styles, and she bought a straight elegant coat-dress in champagne silk, with brown piping and a pure white collar. Shelley's was full-skirted, to emphasise her slim waist, and the material was fine turquoise lawn, with embroidery at the collar and cuffs. Constance Richards stood nervously, as her dress was wrapped carefully in tissue paper. 'You really do think I made the right choice?' she asked anxiously.

'You looked like a film star.' Rosie had an open cheerful face that couldn't lie. 'Black and white stripes, and that gorgeous white hat with the red rose at the brim. Don't you feel good in it?'

'I must confess I do. But I haven't bothered with dresses for so long—it brings back some happy memories of my young days. I'd forgotten, it was so long ago, that I did have some happy days among the bad ones.'

Shelley said quickly, 'And think of the future. The days to come are what matters, not what has past.'

A masculine voice from the doorway answered her. 'How very true, Shelley. The future is what really matters. We can't change the past, but we can all do our best to make the future perfect.'

His eyes were on her, but Shelley wasn't ready for any attempts at reconciliation. Coolly she said, 'Good morning, Miguel. We've just finished here. Did you come for anything?'

'Yes, unfortunately. I've come to see what Victoria's bill is this month. She's an extravagant girl, but I suppose given her looks, it is only natural to make the most of herself.'

'Yes, you really ought to pay her more, Miguel,' said Shelley coldly. 'Then she could afford to buy her own clothes.'

'Ah, yes. You think it odd that I pay her bills? It is part of a rather complicated arrangement that has been going on for a few years now.'

'Really?' Shelley sounded bored. 'Well, we must be off. Your domestic arrangements are nothing to do with us, Dr Rafaelo.' And she swept out, followed by Rosie and Constance Richards.

It was Mrs Richards who commented. 'My, Shelley, you were rather abrupt with that nice young man.'

Shelley said, 'It really isn't what it looks like.'

'I know, my dear. You and the good doctor are thick as thieves, and I can't think of a better man for you.'

'I can.' Shelley didn't feel she could face this kind of conversation. 'You must excuse me — I promised to go along to the tennis courts. Will you take my dress with you to the villa, Rosie?'

'Yes, sure. Aren't you coming for lunch with Mrs Richards?'

'No, thanks all the same. I must go. See you later.'

Shelley wandered round the apartment blocks, in the shade of the abundant trees and shrubs so well arranged about the complex. After she had given Miguel time to pay the bills and get away, she retraced her steps and found herself a table at a café in an arcade in one of the ornamental squares by a pretty fountain. She ordered a cold beer in a tall glass, and sat quietly, watching the rainbows in the fountain. Someone sat opposite to her, hiding the view, and Miguel said, 'Did you enjoy your little walk? You weren't expected at the tennis courts at all, were you?'

'Your detective skills amaze me,' she said with heavy sarcasm. 'I really don't know why you bother following me.' Miguel looked at her with his calm, aristocratic eyes, and she had the grace to feel a little ashamed of herself. 'I'm sorry, I shouldn't have said that. I'm——'

'I know how you feel, and I know I caused it. I'm sorry too. I only came over because our strategy has succeeded with Lopez and I was so pleased I wanted to tell you about it. If you like you can come back to Casa Madrid and see for yourself.' And when she opened her mouth to refuse Miguel said, 'Put it like this, then—I've found an effective treatment for a joiner with cancerphobia, and it might be helpful for your career to see exactly how it works.'

The waiter brought a second beer and set it before Miguel. He took a deep draught, and wiped his brow with the back of his hand, taking the spectacles off to polish them with a white handkerchief. Shelley stole a glance at his face, this face that was so familiar, yet she had not recognised it when it belonged to an imaginary man called Miguelito. He looked up suddenly and their eyes met. She said hurriedly, 'Thanks for the invitation. I'll come over later—I'll make my own way.'

'But I can easily take you and bring you back.'

'No—thanks all the same.'

'Oh, Shelley——'

'I'll see you later, then.' She got up, leaving her glass untouched, and walked away rapidly. She didn't want to see the hurt in his eyes, in case it made her soften and forgive him. She didn't want to forgive him. He had played the worst of tricks on her, making her lose all her self-respect, and it was something that would rankle in her heart for the rest of her life.

Rosie was resting on the couch when Shelley went in. 'I hung your dress up,' she said. 'There's ham and bread in the fridge.'

'I'm not hungry.'

'Shelley, I was meaning to ask you—do you know who Miguelito is? Did you find out his secret?'

'I'm not saying anything at all about him.'

'But he's left Samana. Everyone knows — Pepe says he's going on a foreign tour and won't be back for months. Surely you can tell me now?'

Shelley went out to the patio and sat on the swing. 'The man took me into his confidence. I can't break it, just because he's out of the country. Anyway, he didn't tell me when I met him. I found out later.'

Rosie didn't pursue her questions, much to Shelley's relief. She said, 'It's funny, isn't it? When you came here, you said you were going to find out about him, and you succeeded. It's amazing, really, considering how many girls have longed to do what you did.'

'Rosie, keep all this to yourself or I'll strangle you personally. I want to forget all I ever knew about precious Miguelito.'

'That's sad, Shelley. Really sad, because you loved him so much at first.'

'I loved a fantasy. The real thing isn't quite as loveable.'

'Did he —— ?'

'Don't say another word, or your body won't be in a fit state to wear your champagne silk dress!'

Rosie subsided in giggles.

Shelley drove to Casa Madrid later, not to please Miguel, but because she was inwardly delighted that his plan had worked with regard to Señor Lopez. It was a simple strategy, to give the patient something to keep him occupied. It had yet to be seen if the carpenter would relapse after the wedding was over. But as she climbed from the jeep, she stood in wonder at the magnificent edifice being constructed with workmanlike efficiency.

The helpers had gone for a siesta, but Lopez still worked, carving the branches into intricate shapes, with dozens of little crannies where pots of flowers could be sited. Shelley stood watching him for a while before he noticed her, and he came down to greet her. 'It's good to have something to do,' he told her.

'But you had your business before. How does making this differ from having orders from the public?'

'I suppose because it's such a happy occasion. Little Lina—all the village knows Lina and Pablo—sweethearts since they were eleven!'

'So doing this has given you your appetite back?'

'I'm eating my wife's cooking!'

'And you'll do your share at the wedding, I hope.'

'Yes, yes, I will.' He looked up at the archway. 'I must get back to work. It must be finished by Friday.'

'I'm delighted to see you looking so well. Don't let yourself sink so low again—come and talk to me or to the doctor. And remember all those negative tests.'

'I will, *señorita*—and thank you again. See you at the wedding.'

Shelley walked away. It was all very quiet around the villa, and she assumed everyone was having a siesta. She wandered for a while under the climbing roses and clematis, coiled over wooden trellises to make shady walkways. There was a rustic seat on an area of crazy paving looking out towards the neat lawns. There were fruit trees beyond the grass, and then the fields themselves, and the terraces of tomatoes, vegetables and vines. Birds nestled quietly in the shade, and a peacock and peahen sought the cool of the tiled patio under a colonnade of marble.

Then she saw him. Close to the peacocks, Miguel lay, fast asleep on a sofa-swing shaded by its canopy. Amazingly innocent and vulnerable in sleep, his handsome face charmed her out of her bad mood, and she stood transfixed, unable to look away. Poor Miguel, he must be tired. Yet he managed his estate as well as the complex with extraordinary energy and good humour. And still he found time to heal the sick. He wasn't a bad man. He treated everyone with courtesy and thoughtfulness. Everyone, that was, except

Shelley Cameron, whom he duped into making herself appear silly, into opening her mouth to reveal her inner self, thinking she was talking to someone else. Oh, Miguel, how could you do it? How could you hurt me like that? She looked down at his sleeping form for what seemed like hours. It reminded her of the time she had slept here, and woken to find him beside her with his arm around her in his beautifully furnished bedroom.

How could someone as good-looking as Miguel do something so lowdown and mean? Maybe he didn't mean to. Maybe it had happened too quickly? Yet he it was who had set up a meeting with 'Miguelito' quite deliberately, knowing that he was going to dupe her into going. Oh, no, he meant it all right.

'Shelley, is that you?' He had rolled over just a little, and opened his eyes.

'Yes. I've seen Lopez and I'm just going.' She turned and started to walk, but he caught up with her with those lithe strides of his, and took her roughly into his arms. She was given no time to protest, as he found her mouth with his, and pressed her hard against him. She clenched her fists, unable to struggle, but determined not to give him the satisfaction of knowing she wanted him. Somehow her own anger and his frustration together turned into a mutual all-embracing passion, and they clung together, hating and loving at the same time. 'Let — me — go!' she panted. And he loosed his grip suddenly, and stood back with an oath, his hand going up to his lip where blood appeared at the site of her teeth-marks.

He took his hand away and looked at the smear of red blood on his fingers. They faced each other, their breath coming in gasps, while, oblivious to the humans on the patio, two hummingbirds whistled as they nestled together in the branches of a scarlet hibiscus. Shelley suddenly swung on her heel and ran down towards her jeep, her breath coming in searing sobs as she ran. She started the engine and turned the jeep so that its tyres squealed, then drove back down the drive and down the pretty hillside, wanting only to be somewhere by herself to sit and mourn.

Constance Richards was her passenger in the jeep on Saturday, as they made their way to the little church of Santa Barbara. Shelley hadn't seen Miguel or heard from him since their meeting at Casa Madrid. She managed to conceal her feelings from those around her, however, and she was doubly encouraging to her passenger, who, uncharacteristically for her, was nervous about the wedding. 'You see, Shelley, there's so much of me that I thought was dead, coming alive in this place. I'd trained myself to have no feelings — yet suddenly I'm coming back to life. I'm not sure if I've done the right thing.'

'I'm the one who made you come.'

'I could have refused,' said the old lady, reasonably. 'No, Shelley. I made this bed, and I've got to lie on it.'

'Well, you have a very pretty outfit to do it in.'

'Do you really think so? I don't look totally ridiculous?'

'Not a bit of it. You look like the lady you are.'

The village was decked with flags and flowers, with garlands of leaves between the trees and over the doors of all the cottages, and the villagers were all out in the street, the children playing in their best white frilled dresses and shirts. The handful of people from the complex, including Rosie and Francisco, stood together in a group, waiting for the bride to come out of her grandfather's cottage. Shelley and Constance walked over to stand with them. They could hear the sound of music coming nearer, and everyone turned as a silver band came round the corner into the main dusty street, men dressed in grey trousers and pink shirts, their instruments glistening in the morning sun.

They strode along bravely, and the tune they played was 'Can't Buy Me Love'.

And then Abuelo came out of the cottage, dressed in a light grey suit, with a carnation in his buttonhole. His steel-grey hair was neatly combed, and he stood with great pride acknowledging the cheers of the onlookers. His eyes roved round the scene, and Shelley heard Constance draw in her breath with a little sob. She looked round quickly in case Constance was ill, but she was smiling through two tears trickling down her cheeks, and her eyes were very bright. 'I'm glad I've seen him again,' she whispered.

Abuelo Freitas stood to attention as Lina came out, a vision of beauty in a froth of lace and tulle and fresh flowers. She smiled and waved, then took her grandfather's arm to walk the few hundred yards to the church. Slowly the entire village followed them, moving with great dignity and a great swell of happiness.

Then Miguel Rafaelo appeared among them, dressed in a grey morning suit, a white carnation in his buttonhole, and it was Shelley's turn to turn pale and draw in a gasp of air as though afraid she might faint. Miguel smiled and greeted those nearest to him, and fell into step beside Lopez, bending to speak a few words quietly to him and his wife. Shelley felt her lip tremble, but she couldn't get away now. Constance was clutching her arm, and they were almost at the church.

Lina, her mother Dolores, and old Abuelo stood at the door as the congregation filed in, gossiping and excited, as the band played and the organist competed with it. Lina squealed with delight when she saw Constance and Shelley. '*Mamá, Abuelo, aqui esta mi señora!*'

Constance's grip almost stopped the circulation in Shelley's arm as they paused in front of the Freitas family. The old lady, her white hat with its red rose trembling, looked into the eyes of the old soldier, Felipe Freitas. His look was interested at first, but something in her made him look again. There was a look of great disbelief on the old face, turning slowly to realisation. 'Constanza?'

She nodded. But the congregation was urging them on, and the priest was waiting, and they were borne inwards by the crush of people. Shelley found tears in her own eyes, as Constance sat with a beatific look on her face, and young Pablo, looking neat and dapper in his best clothes, stood smiling at the altar, waiting for his childhood sweetheart to join him.

Miguel had provided a carriage and pair for the newly-weds, and they had the privilege of riding up to Casa Madrid, where they rested and freshened up while the rest of the guests walked up the hill. But the scene that awaited them was worth the walk. The couple sat under Lopez's archway, smothered in flowers. The gardens were garlanded with coloured lights, and the silver band, having refreshed its members while the marriage took place, played with gusto as the guests were all received. Maids took trays of drinks round, and a great banquet was placed on rows of tables that covered one whole side of the lawn.

Shelley was sitting with Constance. 'He said he'd come and speak to me later.'

'You're not nervous any more?'

'No, Shelley, it's the best thing I ever did. To think that after all these years he's alive and well, and I can — oh, talk to him and touch him. I used to weep buckets because I wanted to touch him again.'

'You'll be able to visit like old friends now. Any time you want.'

Constance put her hand on Shelley's arm. 'Shelley, don't let me have another heart attack! Oh, how glad I am that I didn't die. Thank you for looking after me so well. I want to live — just a few more months, just to have time to catch up on old times.'

Miguel had been walking round, chatting to guests. Shelley had been conscious of him through the corner of her eye, but had deliberately made no effort to speak to him. What could she say to someone she had been so close to, had spoken so bitterly to? And to Miguel of all people, who together with Constance Richards was responsible for making this wedding the event of the century in Santa Barbara. He was getting closer. He would have to speak to them. Just then Constance said, 'Excuse me, Shelley, I must just go and speak to Lina—she's beckoning me.' And suddenly Shelley was sitting by herself and Miguel was turning towards her.

They stood facing one another. No words would come. Then Miguel said in a strangled sort of voice, 'When all I want to do is get blind drunk, I have to play the host. Life's not very fair, is it, Shelley?' And he moved on.

She sat down again, staring into space, hearing the bitterness in his voice and full of inner urges willing her to go to him and apologise. But she couldn't. And as the bridal couple stood up for the first dance, she felt the enormous gulf between their obvious carefree happiness and her present misery. She and Miguel both. Other couples were joining in now. There was a cheer as Abuelo Freitas and Constance Richards stood up together. Shelley watched them. To the rest of the guests, they were just an old couple getting to know one another. Only Shelley, Rosie and Miguel knew what a momentous day this was for them. Suddenly Shelley couldn't see, and she realised that it was her tears that had blinded her.

'In here.' Miguel showed her a side door. 'You don't want to spoil other people's fun.'

'Sorry.'

'Come out when you feel better.' He turned to go.

She burst out, 'You had your fun at my expense! I hope you're satisfied!'

'You know I'm not.' He left her to weep, in a little bower where the gardener kept his seedlings. After a while she couldn't cry any more. Drained and empty, she sat until the redness had faded from her eyes. Then she applied more make-up, and lifted her chin, ready to carry on the act of being happy.

'Shelley, where've you been? Come and dance. Miguel, you haven't danced with Shelley.' And against her will, she found herself in Miguel's arms.

'It's a pretty dress,' he said.

'Thank you. I bought it the day you were paying Victoria's bills.'

He said nothing. He swung her round to the happy music, and his hand held her close, but there was no lightness in their steps. When a servant came up with the telephone, and apologised for breaking up the dancing couple, he couldn't know how relieved they both were. They moved to the side of the patio, and Miguel took the call. 'It's Samana — stomach pains and heavy bleeding. I'll go.'

Shelley grabbed at his arm. 'No, let me. You shouldn't leave your guests.'

He looked at her for a moment, then decided. 'All right, but phone me if you aren't happy with the patient.'

'I'll do that.'

Relieved to be away from the desperate depth of emotion that surrounded Miguel, Shelley ran to the jeep and drove quickly back to the complex. The patient was a girl of about eighteen. She was crying. 'It's just period pain, Nurse, but I don't usually have such a bad time.'

'Try to relax, Anna. Lie back, and I'll give you something for the pain. But tell me, is it possible that you might be pregnant?'

'Pregnant?' Anna thought for a while. 'It — is possible, Nurse.'

'You have a steady boyfriend?'

'Yes.'

'But he's not with you?'

'No — I came with a girl friend. Oh, what shall I do, Nurse? I might be losing a baby, you mean?'

'That was my first thought. I'll have to do a pregnancy test, but until we get the result, I think it safer to keep you in bed.'

'But I'm on holiday!'

'You don't want a pregnancy? It interferes with your plans?'

The girl was silent. 'I never even thought about things like that. I'll stay in bed, Nurse, if you say so.'

'Good girl.' Shelley gave her an injection, and soon the violence of her stomach pains eased. 'You can stay in your own apartment, but I do advise keeping as still and quiet as possible.'

'It's been a shock. Please will you come and see me again?'

'Of course, just as soon as I get the results from this test. And you only have to telephone if you need me.'

'I can't tell you how much better I feel after talking to someone like you.'

Shelley waited for a while alone in the clinic. It was getting dark now, but she couldn't be bothered putting the lights on. She hadn't filled in a card for Anna, but somehow it was too much trouble. Everything was too much trouble.

When the phone rang she was almost in a trance. She picked it up automatically. '*Hola*?'

His voice was quiet. 'Have you dealt with the patient?'

'Yes, Miguel.' She could hear the sound of music in the background. 'I think it was a threatened abortion, so I've sent a sample for pregnancy test, and given her a shot of analgesic.'

'Good.' There was pain and disappointment behind the prosaic words. 'Are you coming back? Lina was asking where you are.'

'I'm too tired. I wouldn't be much use at a party.'

'It went well, your planned meeting of Constanza and Felipe. They have been together all day.'

'I'm very relieved about that.'

'Are you going to treat me like this for the next ten years?'

'Are you even considering going ahead with that contract?'

'I don't break my word, Shelley, whatever other faults you say I have. You can have your contract if you still want it.' There was a pause. He said, 'Shelley? Are you still there?'

She said wearily, 'I'll be in the villa if you need me. Goodnight.'

His voice was very low. 'Goodnight, Shelley.'

She locked the medical centre and emerged into a typically jolly Saturday night. This time last week it had been, last Saturday, when she and Miguel had spent some time together and she was as happy as she had ever been in her life — until that moment when she discovered just how much of a fool he had made of her...

CHAPTER TWELVE

THE following two weeks were two of the most difficult of Shelley's life. They were made bearable only because Rosie and Francisco were so happy that they didn't notice her moods. And the entire staff and management committee at Monte Samana were bubbling over with the news that old Mrs Richards had a boyfriend.

Constance spent all her time down at the village of Santa Barbara. 'They all think I'm his new fancy woman,' she confided to Shelley. 'I don't mind what they think. I've found him again. We've lived such different lives, Shelley, but the moment we were together it didn't matter at all. Never ever say that hope is gone, my dear. If anyone had given up hope in life, it was I.'

Shelley agreed. 'When I met you, you were ready to die. If that isn't giving up hope, I don't know what is.'

'I've invited Felipe up to my villa for dinner. Of course I'll get the restaurant to cater, but I want it to be intimate—just the two of us on the balcony. Oh, Shelley, I'm as excited as a schoolgirl. Will you come and check the details—make sure I haven't forgotten anything?'

'I'll be very happy to.'

'You don't sound your usual happy self. It isn't boyfriend trouble, is it? I'm sure you're too nice a person ever to have boyfriend trouble.'

Shelley said ruefully, 'Nice? Constance, if only you knew me!'

'Well, never mind. Come to the villa in about an hour.'

'How's Felipe getting here?'

'That dear sweet boy Miguel is giving him a lift.'

'Dear sweet boy?'

'What did you say, dear?'

'Nothing. I'll be along in an hour.' But not if that dear sweet boy is anywhere around...

It was touching to see the preparations Constance — and her new maid — had gone to. The table was set with lace mats. A silver candlestick was waiting to be lit and a tiny bowl held red rosebuds. Champagne was already on ice, and best crystal glasses shimmered and winked in the fading sunlight.

'Do you think he'll propose?'

Constance smiled. 'Who knows?' She looked at Shelley and her eyes shone with happiness and fun. 'Maybe mine will be the next wedding in the church of Santa Barbara.' She giggled, and called the maid to bring the best Madeiran embroidered napkins. 'That will do — you may go home now. I'll manage myself.'

'You sure you don't want me to check with the restaurant again before I go, *señora*?'

'I don't think so. I've confirmed the order three times already.'

The girl poured two glasses of sherry, and the old woman sat with the young one and talked about love as the sun sank behind the hill. Shelley, unable to think about much else, said, 'Miguel's a great guy really, isn't he?'

'He's the nicest young man I've ever met.'

'You know he was Miguelito?'

'Who? Oh, that singer fellow. I never went myself. Was he good?' Constance made it seem so unimportant.

'He was magnificent. But he was only Miguel acting.'

'How quaint. I can't see how he finds the time, with all his other activities. He'll have to slow down when he marries.'

'Yes.' When Victoria grew just a little bit older and

wiser, and knew how to manage a household as well as a medical centre.

'He ought to marry soon,' said Constance. 'I see a wistfulness in him, and I think it's because subconsciously he wants a son to be a friend to him, to carry on his name and help him in his work.'

Shelley said thoughtfully, 'Yes, maybe you're right. He needs someone — he's always alone whenever you come across him.'

There was a knock at the front door, and Shelley jumped up to open it. Abuelo Freitas stood there, and his hands and face were smeared with dust. 'What is it? Come in, come in.'

Constance came hurrying as fast as she could with her stick. 'Felipe, what's the matter? Where's Miguel?'

'He's down at the roundabout. There's been a bad accident and he's helping with the injured. The ambulances are there. There's nothing anyone can do. I hope you don't mind me coming, but he told me I should come on up.'

Shelley said, 'I'd better go and see. It's nice to see you, Abuelo. Come in and make yourself comfortable.'

'Yes, come in, Felipe. . .' Constance stood there in a simple white dress, and in the twilight she looked like a slim young girl holding out welcoming arms to her guest. The old man crossed the room to her, and Shelley went out, quietly closing the door behind her. A miracle had happened, and time had gone backwards.

She jumped into the jeep and drove furiously down the hill. As soon as she passed the gate she could hear the sirens of ambulances echoing round the valley, and see the flashing lights of the emergency vehicles. She parked on a verge some distance away and ran to the roundabout. The grass in the middle had been ploughed up into a dustbowl, and here and there pools of dark blood showed where bodies thrown out had lain before being taken away to hospital.

Her mouth dry with urgency, she ran up to an ambulanceman, shouting in Spanish, 'Can I help? I'm a nurse.'

'Please come to the hospital. You have a vehicle? There are many casualties, and we need the staff.'

Thankful that because of Rosie's appendix she knew the quickest way to the hospital well, Shelley drove like a demon after the ambulance, and ran in as the casualty was stretchered in. Quickly introducing herself to the sister-in-charge, she looked around for the nearest unattended patient. He was dead, and she drew the sheet over his face before turning her attention to the next. Everywhere doctors and nurses were bending over prostrate forms, and shouting orders and instructions.

Shelley found herself with a woman whose slashed arm required urgent suturing. Finding a junior nurse to assist, between them they cleaned and disinfected the arm, and applied a tight tourniquet above the wound. As she caught the jagged edges of skin together with as delicate a stitch as she could—the patient was a young woman, and a scar was the last thing she would want—Shelley said, 'That roundabout is terribly dangerous. Everyone has known about it for years.'

The nurse agreed. 'These unfortunate people have come from the north, and they do not know the road as we do.'

Someone in a white coat came up to them. 'I'm a doctor. Do you need any help?'

'I can manage here, Doctor. Go to the next one——' Shelley looked up, suddenly recognising that deep reliable voice. 'Go to the next bed, Miguel. This is only a suturing. She has no other injuries, thank God.'

For a moment their eyes met. '*Sí*, Shelley. . .' And he was gone.

The little nurse asked, as she handed Shelley a fresh needle and silk suture, 'You know him?'

'I work for him.'

It was almost morning when the last of the accident victims was warded. Two were still in emergency surgery, but the worst of the incident was over, and the weary medical staff accepted a welcome cup of coffee before making their way home. She had lost sight of Miguel.

She walked slowly out of the casualty department. Then she found him. He was sitting on a bench, his face and shirt streaked with dirt and dried blood, and he was leaning his head against the wall, his eyes closed. She stopped, her heart full of remorse and sadness and a great, overwhelming love. Gently she shook him by the shoulder, and his eyes opened. His voice was hoarse with exhaustion. 'Shelley, you have the jeep? I came in an ambulance with a patient—I had to do an emergency tracheotomy before we got to hospital.'

'Did he survive?'

'Yes. I saved his life.'

'Let's go home, then.'

Miguel closed his eyes again in the jeep. With full heart, Shelley drove through the silent, magic dawn, looking at him sideways from time to time. As they left the confines of the city and started on the long straight empty road to Samana, the sun was glowing ruby-red behind the dark wooded hills, the sky translucent delicate silk. She said quietly, with only the noise of the engine as accompaniment, 'I want to apologise, sincerely apologise, for being so childish and stupid and rude to you. It was foolish hurt pride that made me behave so coldly towards you. After tonight, I realise that real life is what matters. Real life, and acceptance of what we have. You taught me that, Miguel. Ever since we met, my dear, so gently and subtly you've been teaching me, you and

Miguelito, and instead of thanking you I had this attack of childish pique and blamed you for hurting my feelings! They needed hurting, Miguel—I needed to grow up. Well, I've grown up tonight, and it's too late—too late for us, but at least I've had the chance of putting things straight with you, and that puts my mind at peace.'

She looked at him again. His eyes were still closed, and she smiled at her own foolishness. 'Asleep, my darling Miguel? It's just as well. I know I've lost you. It's such an empty feeling, you know. I know I've lost my chance of happiness, and I deserve to. But when I saw you tonight, working so desperately to save lives and help people, I knew exactly how deeply and hopelessly I do love you. I don't know how I had the nerve to speak to you as I did—to turn you away when you were being so nice and so good. I must have been out of my mind. I know I was, and it took a tragedy like this to make me see straight.' She paused and looked at his dear face again. He stirred and took a deep breath in his sleep. Her voice low and full of emotion, she went on, 'Take no notice of me rambling away like this, dear, dear Miguelito. It helps to ease my pain, even though you aren't hearing me. I'll come and say goodbye when you're rested. I know you won't want me to stay. I just know it, even though you're too nice to say it to my face.'

She didn't turn in at Monte Samana, but went on, past the mess of rutted dirt and blood-stained grass that was all that was left of the roundabout, fenced off now, with police directing the traffic round it.

Miguel stirred, and said, 'Sorry, did you say something?'

'No.' She whispered the words. 'Sleep again. I'll wake you when we get there.' They drove through the lemon groves, where early workers were just arriving in a lorry to pick the fruit and load it. Santa Barbara village street was deserted, except for Inés just opening up the shop to take in the milk left by the farmer.

Shelley drove into the Casa Madrid grounds, past the ornamental gate flanked by its two tall palm trees, right to the door, where Miguel's servant and cook had already seen the jeep from the window, and stood waiting to help him down. Miguel opened his eyes and shifted in his seat. Then he turned to Shelley, and with a gesture that touched and surprised her by its gentleness, he put up his hand to her cheek. The warmth of his skin against hers made her catch her breath, and she turned her face so that his hand slid away. He murmured, 'Thank you, Shelley. You look so tired—go home and rest.' He got down from the jeep and walked into the villa, his shirt crumpled, and his footsteps weary.

Shelley realised that tears were coursing down her cheeks, and that the cook was watching her. Shyly she said, 'It's been a hard night.'

'Are you sure you are all right, *señorita*? Would you like to come in also, and rest? Take some coffee?'

'No, no, I couldn't do that. I must get back. Good day to you.'

Her eyes were almost closing when she finally drew up outside the villa. Rosie was standing at the door, and ran to help her in. 'There's hot coffee and croissants, then you're to sleep for two days. Doctor's orders!'

'Your orders, you mean!'

'No, doctor's. Miguel telephoned that you were on your way and that you were exhausted.'

'He did?' She was too tired to question this latest example of Miguel's thoughtfulness. She said, 'Seven people died—seven, Rosie! But we saved twelve, and two were in surgery when I left.'

'Don't talk any more. You did all you could. I'm sure you and Miguel helped a lot.'

'He did. He did a tracheotomy in the ambulance.

The patient would have died if Miguel hadn't been with him.' Shelley's hands were clutched tightly round the mug of coffee, and Rosie wisely let her talk it out of her system. She said, 'I apologised to Miguel for being a pig, but he didn't hear me — he was fast asleep, poor darling. I love him so much, Rosie, that I think I won't be able to live without him. But I have to, because there's no way he'll have time for me after what I said to him.' She heard herself talking, but it was almost in her sleep, and her voice gradually trailed away.

She was sitting by the pool. It was two days later, and the news had got round that Miguel and Shelley were heroes. She had even been interviewed and photographed by the local paper. But she hadn't seen Miguel — he had stayed in Santa Barbara. She knew why. He had had enough of Shelley Cameron and her selfish, petty little ways.

Victoria came up. 'Shelley, there's a man in the medical centre with a stomach upset. Shall I just send him along to Rosie's pharmacy for some diarrhoea mixture?'

Shelley smiled up at her. 'You could run this centre on your own, Victoria! No, I'll come and take a look. Not all stomach upsets are due to overeating.' She walked up the smooth grassy knoll to the centre, and examined the patient. She ended up sending him to Rosie's. But at least she could write on the card, 'On examination nothing abnormal detected'. If she had not examined, she would have felt guilty.

Victoria said, 'You are recovered from your exhaustion, Shelley?'

'Yes, thank you.'

'You are very quiet.'

'Yes, I've been thinking. I — don't think I'll be staying on here, Victoria.'

'Oh, but you must. Everyone knows you now — you're part of the team.'

'That's nice to hear. I've loved every minute of being here.' Shelley sighed. 'But there's a time and a place for everything, and it's time I moved on — saw a bit more of your beautiful country — maybe a bit of the world too, who knows?'

Victoria's big eyes looked even bigger when she looked sad. 'Don't go yet. I was hoping——'

The telephone rang and Victoria picked it up. '*Hola? Sí — sí — sí — OK — adiós.*'

'Who was that?'

'It was Uncle. He wants you to go up to the villa.' Victoria's voice was curious. 'Something about getting your final bonus... You told him you're leaving, then?'

'Uncle who, Victoria?'

'Uncle Miguel.'

Something exploded in Shelley's head. 'I didn't know he was your uncle.' She found herself smiling suddenly. Being her uncle would account for him paying her bills! But then her smile faded — Miguel was still lost to Shelley, even if Victoria no longer proved to be a rival.

'Oh, yes, my mother is his older sister. Miguel promised to look after me for a year while I got some business experience before going to university.'

'That explains why he's so fond of you — why you go there so often.' The girls smiled at each other. Everything was so much clearer now...

Victoria said, 'And why he asked me not to call him uncle in front of you because it made him sound old!'

'No! Did he really do that?'

'He did, honestly. And he asked me to telephone him while you were at the Casa Madrid, and pretend I was Miguelito.'

'That was you!'

'I'm sorry, Shelley, but he really was quite dotty

about you. He needed to fall in love again. I hope you aren't angry with me.'

'Not angry, dear, no. It's been so nice working with you.' Impulsively Shelley went over and hugged Victoria. 'When do I have to go up to Casa Madrid?'

'This evening after work. Oh, I do hope you change your mind about staying. I'm sure he'll try and persuade you.'

'Don't hold your breath,' said Shelley, miserably knowing that persuading her to stay was the very last thing Miguel Rafaelo would do.

She spent some time choosing what to wear to say goodbye. It was depressing looking through her clothes, and remembering the good times she had spent wearing some of these dresses and blouses. She chose a dark green fitted dress—not quite in mourning, but a sombre colour to match her mood. It didn't occur to her that it showed off her pretty fair hair to perfection, and did wonders for her figure.

She drove past the café, and waved to Pablo, and to Lina's two brothers with him. Outside the Freitas cottage Abuelo sat on his usual rocking chair, and beside him sat Constance, also rocking, dressed in old cotton trousers and a loose shirt with the sleeves rolled up. The two old people were deep in conversation.

Shelley braked and stopped. They looked up at her, and it was clear without anything being said that they were doing their best to cram fifty years of living into the next week or two. 'You're well?'

They both replied with vigorous nods and smiles. Dolores came out of the cottage with mugs of coffee for them. 'Here you are, Abuela,' she said to Constance. 'I hope you like it black.'

'I like it the way Abuelo has his.'

Dolores laughed and shook her head. 'I don't know, you two!' She turned to Shelley. 'You will have coffee with us?'

'No, thank you. I just stopped to say good day to these two young things!'

'I tell you, Shelley, they are worse than my Lina was, and Pablo! But so sweet — at least Abuelo has a hobby to take his mind off his old pipe!'

'So much better for your health, Abuelo,' said Shelley, bending and kissing them both. 'See you soon.'

She drove up the hill and stopped the jeep outside the blue and white gateway flanked by its sentinel palm trees, and those two big blue flowerpots, almost as tall as herself. The villa looked welcoming, with its wooden seats and bright red geraniums, the lawns beyond streaked with the long shadows of the cypresses and casuarinas as the sun went down. Slowly Shelley started the engine again, and drove the jeep into the little paved courtyard.

For a moment she stood, uncertain where to go. She felt an aura of sadness around her like a pall. She could hardly bear to think she would never see this pretty place again, nor speak with the cheerful villagers, drink beer in María's café and get hugs from the children when she saw them in Miguel's clinic.

Then Miguel himself came round the corner of the villa, dressed in a white open-necked shirt and dark fitted trousers. Shelley felt the familiar pang of heartache and lost love as their eyes met. He didn't smile. 'Come through, Shelley.'

She was glad it was to be a businesslike parting. She didn't want to cry any more — enough tears had been shed already. 'Victoria said you wanted me to come.'

'Yes.' He led the way to the patio at the back overlooking the shady lawn. The peacocks wandered poetically by, the cock's tail and plumage brilliant in the last rays of the sun. Beside two chairs was a small table, with a jug of wine and two glasses. 'Sit down, Shelley.' He poured the wine, and the sun shone through it, making a pink shadow on the seat. 'You have recovered after the other night?'

'Yes, thank you.'

'I asked you here because you are due a bonus.'

'Is that because I'm leaving?'

'Are you leaving? I haven't been told.'

She said, 'Come on, Miguel—I think we both know I can't stay on.'

'Then it's your choice. I keep to my word, and I offered you a contract. Are you telling me you don't want it?'

She nodded, not trusting herself to speak.

'What about the bonus?'

Shelley swallowed the lump in her throat and said hoarsely, trying to be businesslike, 'I'll accept that, because I thought instead of flying home I'd like to hire a car and drive up to the north—see something of the rest of the country.' Her voice was very steady, monotonous and unemotional, and she was proud of herself for not giving in.

Miguel poured more wine, and took a drink before saying coolly, 'That won't be possible, I'm afraid, because the bonus isn't in cash.'

Annoyed slightly, she turned to face him. 'What is it, then?'

'It's me—as your husband—if you'll have me.' The mask had cracked, and his beloved face was smiling broadly. He took his glasses off and put them on the table, and his eyes were dancing as she hadn't seen them dance since the night he had revealed the identity of Miguelito. 'Will you, Shelley?' He reached across to take her hand.

'I—but—yes, yes, I will, I will, but——'

'Darling, I wasn't completely asleep when you drove me home. I heard all those beautiful things you said to me. I kept quiet because I wanted you to go on talking. It was so beautiful to hear you say those words. I could scarcely believe it. My heart was bursting to reply, but

I was greedy—I wanted to hear more.' He paused, his voice breaking for a moment. 'And you blamed yourself too much. I *was* crass and thoughtless to spring it on you as I did. I deserved your anger. Darling, believe me, *mi querida*, when you're as much in love as I am, you don't always behave rationally. But I'll do my best to change.'

She clung to his hand as though someone might take him away again. 'So will I.'

'I don't want you to change. I want you just as you are. Come here.' And she was on his knee, and their arms were round each other, and though the sun had gone down the garden at that moment was glorious, full of a blaze of splendour that surrounded them like a halo.

Shelley said, kissing the top of his head between words, 'Constance said you looked like a man who needed a son.'

Miguel looked up at her so that she could reach his lips with hers. 'A son? Sounds like a good idea to me. Any ideas what we should call him?'

She started to smile, and they both said the name together, ending with an explosion of laughter, and Shelley almost falling off his knee—'Miguelito!'

He stood up and steadied her. They looked into one another's eyes, and kissed with a great tenderness, as though they had to make up for the anger last time. He whispered, 'Come on in. There's champagne in the fridge, and I'm sure I can find something to eat.'

'Why? Can't Fernanda get it?'

'I—sent the servants away for tonight.'

She smiled again. 'I feel as though I'm floating on air. Hold my hand, Miguel, in case I get blown away!' They were inside the lounge now, with soft lights, and the delicate curtains blowing in a slight breeze.

Miguel picked up his guitar from where it was lying on the sofa so that she could sit down. As he stood before her holding it, they started to laugh again. He flung the guitar on to a chair, and bent down to pick Shelley up bodily instead, lifting her as though she weighed nothing at all. Holding her against him, he whispered, 'Shall we leave the cabaret till later, darling?'

'Much later.' Shelley put both arms round his neck. He was hers, and she would never get used to the glory of it. 'Miguel?'

'Yes, I am here.'

'Miguel — I love you.'

He carried her upstairs and laid her, kissing her, on the bed. For a while they didn't speak, then he whispered, 'When you walked into my office that very first day, *querida*, the sun came in with you. Something hit me inside. I knew then I never wanted you to leave me.'

She stirred in his arms. 'It wasn't very obvious, Miguel.'

'You had those inhibitions — that's why I needed Miguelito for a little while. You were so open about your admiration for him. I knew he could succeed where perhaps you would not believe me.'

She didn't want him to stop kissing her, but curiosity made her murmur, 'Did you honestly believe that I wouldn't be angry with you for telling me so abruptly that you were Miguelito?'

'I was selfish. I was tired of the masquerade myself — it had gone too far without me meaning it. I wanted it to stop. I wanted us to be honest with each other, and I rushed into it, hoping you would understand.'

'And I let you down.'

He held her tightly against the length of him, and there was no space between their bodies. 'No, no, sweet — I deserved all those hard words. I had taken your affection for granted.' He began to kiss her cheek, her ear, her throat, and his words were whispered against her tingling skin. Their clothes rustled as his gentle fingers began to unbutton her dress, and gentle lips explored her body, her breasts that lifted to accept his carresses. 'I'll never take you for granted again. I needed that lesson just as you needed yours. My little Shelley, you are the only woman I have ever met who can make me very happy. Promise you'll never leave me?'

'That's the easiest promise in the world to keep,' she whispered. 'And Miguel, now that I look back on your little masquerade, you know I think I did enjoy it after all!'

He raised himself on to one elbow so that he could look down into her eyes. Her hair was dishevelled over the pillow, and his dark eyes were tender. Outside a nightingale trilled in the casuarina trees, and their leaves rustled in the night air, a sweet overture to love. Miguel smiled. 'You certainly know how to be angry with a man, *querida*—but it was worth it all to hear you apologising, on that journey back from the hospital. It was then I finally knew I had found my bride. My wife and my future.' He stroked back her hair from her face, and bent to kiss her.

MILLS & BOON

CHRISTMAS KISSES...

...THE GIFT OF LOVE

Four exciting new Romances to melt your heart this Christmas from some of our most popular authors.

ROMANTIC NOTIONS — Roz Denny
TAHITIAN WEDDING — Angela Devine
UNGOVERNED PASSION — Sarah Holland
IN THE MARKET — Day Leclaire

Available November 1993   *Special Price only £6.99*

Available from W. H. Smith, John Menzies, Martins, Forbuoys, most supermarkets and other paperback stockists.
Also available from Mills & Boon Reader Service, FREEPOST, PO Box 236, Thornton Road, Croydon, Surrey CR9 9EL. (UK Postage & Packing free)

FOR BETTER
FOR WORSE

An unforgettable story of broken dreams and new beginnings

Penny Jordan is set to take the bestseller lists by storm again this autumn, with her stunning new novel which is a masterpiece of raw emotion.

A story of obsessions...
A story of choices...
A story of love.

LARGE-FORMAT PAPERBACK AVAILABLE FROM NOVEMBER

PRICED: £8.99

WORLDWIDE

*Available from W.H. Smith, John Menzies, Martins, Forbuoys, most supermarkets and other paperback stockists.
Also available from Worldwide Reader Service, Freepost, PO Box 236, Thornton Road, Croydon, Surrey CR9 9EL.
(UK Postage & Packing free)*

Discover the thrill of *Love on Call* with 4 FREE Romances

FREE
BOOKS FOR YOU

In the exciting world of modern medicine, the emotions of true love acquire an added poignancy. Now you can experience these gripping stories of passion and pain, heartbreak and happiness - with Mills & Boon absolutely FREE! AND look forward to a regular supply of *Love on Call* delivered direct to your door.

🌹 🌹 🌹

Turn the page for details of how to claim 4 FREE books AND 2 FREE gifts!

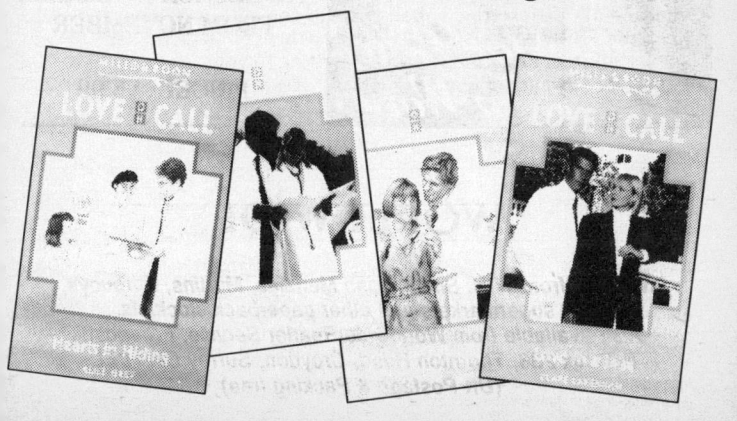

An irresistible offer from Mills & Boon

Here's a very special offer from Mills & Boon for you to become a regular reader of *Love on Call*. And we'd like to welcome you with 4 books, a cuddly teddy bear and a special mystery gift - absolutely FREE and without obligation!

Then, every month look forward to receiving 4 brand new *Love on Call* romances delivered direct to your door for only £1.80 each. Postage and packing is FREE!

Plus a FREE Newsletter featuring authors, competitions, special offers and lots more...

This invitation comes with no strings attached. You may cancel or suspend your subscription at any time and still keep your FREE books and gifts.

It's so easy. Send no money now but simply complete the coupon below and return it today to:

Mills & Boon Reader Service, FREEPOST, PO Box 236, Croydon, Surrey CR9 9EL.

NO STAMP NEEDED

YES! Please rush me 4 FREE *Love on Call* books and 2 FREE gifts! Please also reserve me a Reader Service subscription. If I decide to subscribe, I can look forward to receiving 4 brand new *Love on Call* books for only £7.20 every month - postage and packing FREE. If I choose not to subscribe, I shall write to you within 10 days and still keep the FREE books and gifts. I may cancel or suspend my subscription at any time simply be writing to you.
I am over 18 years of age.   Please write in BLOCK CAPITALS

Ms/Mrs/Miss/Mr _____ EP62D

Address _____

_____

_____ Postcode _____

Signature _____

Offer closes 31st March 1994. The right is reserved to refuse an application and change the terms of this offer. One application per household. Offer not valid to current Love on Call subscribers. Offer valid only in UK and Eire. Overseas readers please write for details. Southern Africa write to IBS, Private Bag, X3010, Randburg, 2125, South Africa. You may be mailed with offers from other reputable companies as a result of this application. Please tick box if you would prefer not to receive such offers. ☐

mps MAILING PREFERENCE SERVICE

ESCAPE INTO ANOTHER WORLD...

...With Temptation Dreamscape Romances

Two worlds collide in 3 very special Temptation titles, guaranteed to sweep you to the very edge of reality.

The timeless mysteries of reincarnation, telepathy and earthbound spirits clash with the modern lives and passions of ordinary men and women.

Available November 1993   Price £5.55

MILLS & BOON

Available from W. H. Smith, John Menzies, Martins, Forbuoys, most supermarkets and other paperback stockists.
Also available from Mills & Boon Reader Service, FREEPOST, PO Box 236, Thornton Road, Croydon, Surrey CR9 9EL. (UK Postage & Packing free)

MILLS & BOON

LOVE ON CALL

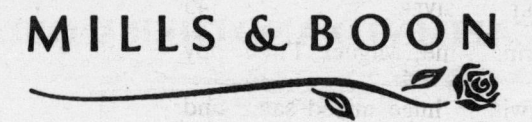

The books for enjoyment this month are:

SWEET DECEIVER Jenny Ashe
VETS IN OPPOSITION Mary Bowring
CROSSMATCHED Elizabeth Fulton
OUTBACK DOCTOR Elisabeth Scott

♥   ♥   ♥   ♥   ♥

Treats in store!

Watch next month for the following absorbing stories:

SECOND THOUGHTS Caroline Anderson
CHRISTMAS IS FOREVER Margaret O'Neill
CURE FOR HEARTACHE Patricia Robertson
CELEBRITY VET Carol Wood

Available from W.H. Smith, John Menzies, Volume 1, Forbuoys, Martins, Tesco, Asda, Safeway and other paperback stockists.

Also available from Mills & Boon Reader Service, Freepost, P.O. Box 236, Croydon, Surrey CR9 9EL.

Readers in South Africa - write to:
Book Services International Ltd, P.O. Box 41654, Craighall, Transvaal 2024.